A Christmas Cthulhu
By David Griffiths

A Christmas Cthulhu
Copyright: David Griffiths
Published: 3rd December 2012
Publisher: David Griffiths
The right of David Griffiths to be identified as author of this Work has been asserted by him in accordance with sections 77 and 78 of the Copyright, Designs and Patents Act 1988.
All rights reserved. No part of this publication may be reproduced, stored in retrieval system, copied in any form or by any means, electronic, mechanical, photocopying, recording or otherwise transmitted without written permission from the publisher. You must not circulate this book in any format.

Dedicated to
Howard Phillips Lovecraft
and
Charles John Huffam Dickens
whose fantastic works inspired these affectionate tributes.

A Christmas Cthulhu
   By David Griffiths

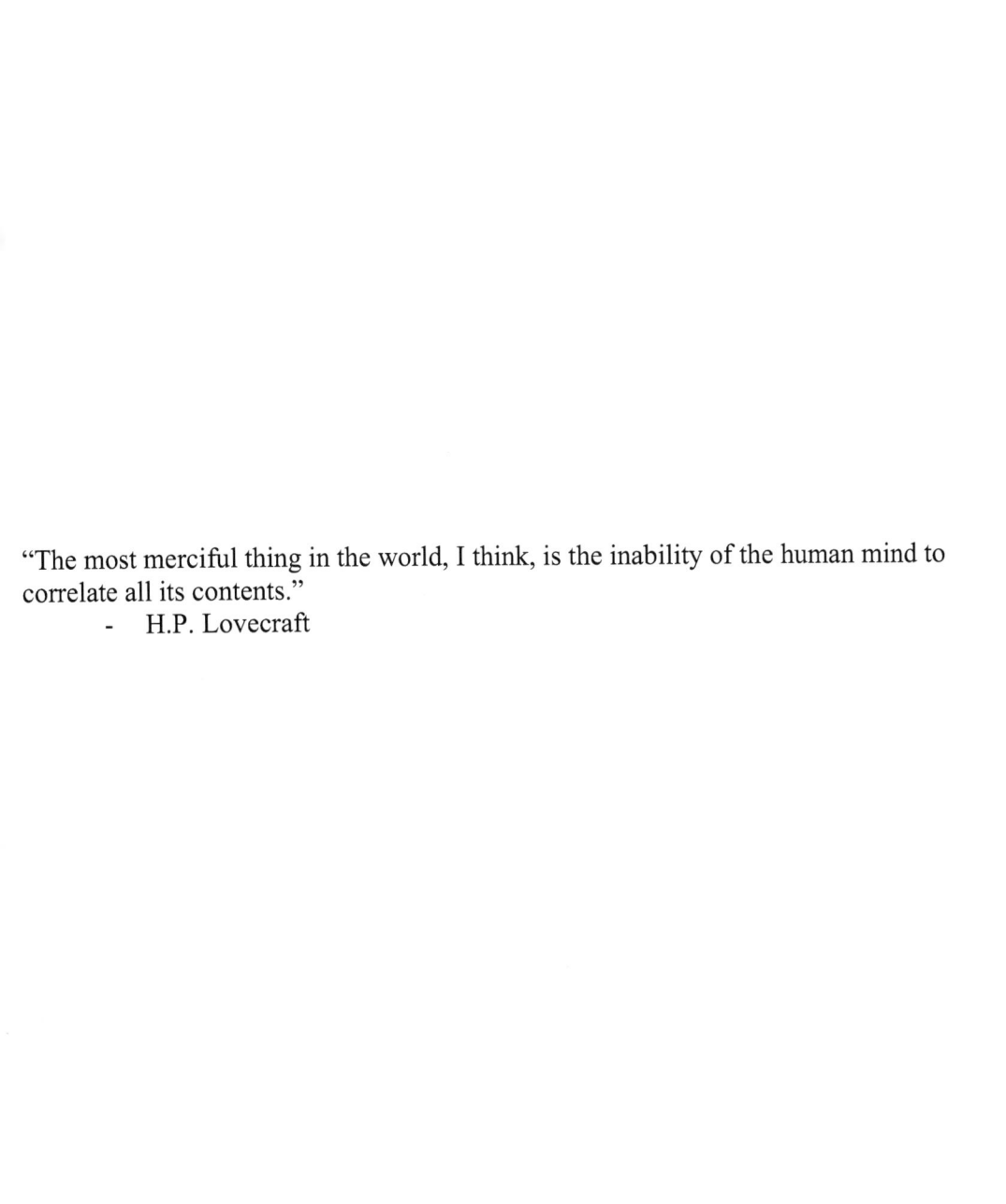

"The most merciful thing in the world, I think, is the inability of the human mind to correlate all its contents."
- H.P. Lovecraft

I

Of the account I am to tell you, I must begin by making one thing abundantly clear. Marley was dead to begin with. He was laid to rest on December 25th 1924 in his home town of Innsmouth. The notification of his death was sent to one of his mourners, Ebenezer Scrooge. You can be certain that for Scrooge to have been contacted, there can be no doubt of the accuracy of Mr Marley's mortality. Indeed, Old Marley was as dead as a door-nail.

Of the relationship between Mr Scrooge and Mr Marley, I can speak thus; their explorations of the Antarctic are hitherto unmatched in their size and scope, their research at Miskatonic University unparalleled. Mr Marley believed that we live on a placid island of ignorance in the midst of black seas of infinity. Had he imparted this wisdom upon Mr Scrooge, he would no doubt have expanded upon his hypothesis, adding that it was not meant that we should voyage far. The sciences have hitherto harmed us little; but some day the piecing together of dissociated knowledge will open up such terrifying vistas of reality, and of our frightful position therein, that we shall either go mad from the revelation or flee from the light into the peace and safety of a new dark age.

Did Scrooge know Marley was dead? Of course he did. How could it be otherwise? Scrooge and he were partners for I don't know how many years at the Miskatonic University. Was Scrooge his sole friend and mourner? There was but one person whom attended the funeral. This person I shall expand upon shortly, but I can assure you it was not Ebenezer Scrooge. This bothered the aforementioned person greatly, being Jacob Marley's sole heir and nephew to Ebenezer Scrooge, but Scrooge was not so dreadfully cut up by the sad event to attend the funeral, for the journey from Arkham to Innsmouth was long and Scrooge could ill afford the time spent away from his research.

I realise my account has so far centred on the question of Mr Marley's mortality. But his death must be distinctly understood for me to truly explain the horror that befell Ebenezer Scrooge on Christmas Eve, 1927. My account is related to you from the recovered journal of Mr Scrooge, my predecessor at the Miskatonic University and first-hand accounts told to me in the aftermath. My superiors forbade me from transcribing the events that led to the death of Mr Scrooge, fearing that the deluded ramblings of a lonely and world weary professor may be taken far more seriously than the University considers. But I intend to defy the ban and speak of those ghastly occurrences before it's too late for me. Besides, the journal which I am to relate might possibly have more than one explanation. I do not know just how much of the whole tale is true, and I have many reasons for not wishing to probe deeper. For my contact with this affair has been closer than that of any other layman, and I have carried away impressions which are yet to drive me to drastic measures.

Scrooge never painted out Old Marley's name from his office door. Sometimes people new to the faculty called Scrooge Scrooge, and sometimes Marley, but he answered to both names. It was all the same to him, for his mind often wandered to places beyond the comprehension of others.

Of Old Scrooge's temperament, I can reveal this; he was hard and sharp as flint, from which no steel had ever struck out generous fire; secret, and self-contained, and solitary as an oyster. None in Miskatonic University, nor Arkham itself, could boast of their love for the man. The cold within him froze his old features, nipped his pointed nose, shrivelled his cheek, stiffened his gait; made his eyes red, his thin lips blue; and spoke out shrewdly in his grating voice. A frosty rime was on his head, and on his eyebrows, and his wiry chin. He carried his own low temperature always about with him; he iced his office in the dog-days; and didn't thaw it one degree at Christmas. External heat and cold had little influence on Scrooge. No warmth could warm, no wintry weather chill him. No wind that blew was bitterer than he, no falling snow was more intent upon its purpose, no pelting rain less open to entreaty. Foul weather didn't know where to have him. The heaviest rain, and snow, and hail, and sleet, could boast of the advantage over him in only one respect. They often came down handsomely, and Scrooge never did. And yet now, in reading the journal of Ebenezer Scrooge – and relaying it to you, my dear reader – I have a semblance of pity for a man whose life was entangled in affairs that his peers would have ridiculed, yet had they seen first-hand as I had, they would have fainted in horror.

Did the people of Arkham know something of Scrooge's plight? Of this I cannot be certain. What I can say is that nobody ever stopped him in the street to say, with gladsome looks, "My dear Scrooge, how are you? When will you come to see me." No beggars implored him to bestow a trifle, no children asked him what it was o'clock, no man or woman ever once in all his life inquired the way to such and such a place, of Scrooge. Even the blindmen's dogs appeared to know his curse; and when they saw him coming on, would tug their owners into doorways and up courts; and then would wag their tails as though they said, "No eye at all is better than an evil eye, dark master! " Was it that Scrooge didn't care? Perhaps he merely remained blissfully ignorant, happy to edge his way along the crowded paths of Arkham life and the bustling corridors of Miskatonic whilst all around him kept their distance.

Old Scrooge's account begins on Christmas Eve, 1927. Ebenezer sat busy in his office. The Arkham winters can be cold and bleak. This particular night I recall was particularly biting and foggy withal. The campus is very nearly deserted on Christmas Eve, save for the office of Mr Scrooge. On the distant city streets of Arkham, people wheezed up and down, beating their hands upon their breasts, and stamping their feet upon the pavement stones to warm them. The city clocks had only just gone three, but it was quite dark already: it had not been light all day: and lights were flaring in the windows of the townhouses. I recall the fog came pouring in at every chink and keyhole, and was so dense without that the houses opposite were mere phantoms. To see the dingy cloud come drooping down, obscuring everything, one might have thought that Nature lived hard by, and was brewing on a large scale.

Scrooge left the door to his office open, so as to keep a watchful eye upon his assistant, who would copy letters and deal with correspondence with regards to funding on behalf of Old Scrooge. Many believed that this clerk, Mr Bob Cratchit, responsible the following day for Mr Scrooge's disappearance. I have visited Bob on several occasions at the asylum and can vouch for him. Though he undoubtedly resented his employer, his part in the downfall of Ebenezer Scrooge was minimal. That is, if reminding Scrooge of the anniversary of his partner's passing could be considered more than a coincidence of what was to come. And I put it to you that this is simply what it was. Sheer unfortunate coincidence.

Footsteps were heard approaching Scrooge's office. The door was flung open to the sounds of "A merry Christmas, uncle! God save you!" This cheery voice belonged to Fred, Scrooge's young nephew. Perhaps you assumed when I spoke of Scrooge's dark intonations that the old miser was without family. I assure you this was not the case. In fact, his family tried so desperately to pull Scrooge back from the brink, as you will no doubt see. This cheery nephew, son to Scrooge's young sister Fan, was a kindhearted soul. Untainted by the lure of the Deep Ones and the secrets kept at the lost city of R'lyeh. But of this I will not speak just now, for their place in this tale will soon become clear.

Scrooge replied to his nephew with a "Bah! Humbug!"

He had so heated himself with rapid walking in the fog and frost, this nephew of Scrooge's, that he was all in a glow; his face was ruddy and handsome; his eyes sparkled, and his breath smoked again.

"Christmas a humbug, uncle!" said Scrooge's nephew. "You don't mean that, I am sure."

"I do," said Scrooge. "Merry Christmas! Bah!"

"Come, then," returned the nephew gaily. "What right have you to be dismal? What reason have you to be morose? You're smart enough."

Scrooge having no better answer ready on the spur of the moment, said, "Bah!" again; and followed it up with "Humbug," before returning to his paperwork.

"Don't be cross, uncle," said the nephew.

"What else can I be," returned the uncle, "when I live in such a world of fools as this. Out upon merry Christmas. What's Christmas time to you but a time for mourning? You arrive at my place of business with a Merry Christmas on your lips, yet it will not return your mother to you. What of her, eh? How easily you forget."

"I do not forget," Fred spoke, gravely, "I have accepted her loss and moved on. I have mourned the loss of my mother and now I must continue to live my life or forever be lost."

"Bah," Scrooge retorted, "You always speak of Fan as though she is gone. Permanently lost to us. But each day I work towards finding and recovering my beloved sister. I know she survived the wreckage and with a fresh diving expedition, I intend to…"

"She was lost, uncle! She has been lost these past ten years despite the best efforts of you and father." Fred referred to Mr Marley. Old Jacob could scarce let go of his wife, just as Old Ebenezer could never mourn for his sister. Many attributed the grief to the death of Jacob Marley. This was only a partial truth. It wasn't grief that killed Mr Marley. If only Scrooge had known, he may have abandoned his foolhardy quest there and then, three years ago.

"If I could work my will," said Scrooge, quickly changing the subject, "every idiot who goes about with "Merry Christmas" on his lips, should be boiled with his own pudding, and buried with a stake of holly through his heart. He should!"

"Uncle!" pleaded the nephew.

"Nephew!" returned Scrooge, sternly, "keep Christmas in your own way, and let me keep it in mine."

"Keep it!" repeated Scrooge's nephew. "But you don't keep it. You mourn it"

"Let me leave it alone, then," said Scrooge. "Much good may it do you! Much good it has ever done you or our family."

"There are many things from which I have derived good, mother used to say," returned the nephew: "Christmas among the rest. But I am sure I have always thought of Christmas time, when it has come round -- apart from the veneration due to its sacred name and origin, if anything belonging to it can be apart from that -- as a good time: a kind, forgiving, charitable, pleasant time: the only time I know of, in the long calendar of the year, when men and women seem by one consent to open their shut-up hearts freely, and to think of people as people, not as another race of creatures bound on other journeys. And therefore, uncle, though it has inadvertently played a part in pain and grief, I believe that it has done me good, and will do me good; and I say, God bless it!"

The clerk, Mr Cratchit, involuntarily applauded. Becoming immediately sensible of the impropriety, he shuffled his paperwork around his desk, dropping his pencil in the process. "Let me hear another sound from you," said Scrooge, " and you'll keep your Christmas by losing your situation. You're quite a powerful speaker, sir," he added, turning to his nephew. "I wonder you don't go into politics."

"Don't be angry, uncle. Come! Dine with us tomorrow."

At this point in Scrooge's journal, he tells of his reply to his nephew. He seemingly goes the full length of the expression, saying he would see him in that extremity first. To those who did not understand Ebenezer Scrooge, they may consider this retort to refer to Hell. Yet, having studied his journal and papers accordingly, it is perhaps more likely to refer to R'lyeh, a lost underwater city in the South Pacific of which Scrooge and Marley devoted great amounts of their academia.

"Why did you get married?" asked Scrooge.

"Because I fell in love."

"Because you fell in love!" growled Scrooge, as if that were the only one thing in the world more ridiculous than a merry Christmas. "May your love bring you more than the sorrow and grief it has brought me these past ten years. Good afternoon!"

"Nay, uncle, but you never came to see me before I married. Why give it as a reason for not coming now? Why fear the love of friends and family?"

"Good afternoon," said Scrooge.

"I want nothing from you; I ask nothing of you; why can't we be friends?"

"Good afternoon," said Scrooge.

"I am sorry, with all my heart, to find you so resolute. We have never had any quarrel, to which I have been a party. But I have made the trial in homage to my mother, your beloved sister. And I make the trial in homage to her love of Christmas, and I'll keep my Christmas humour to the last. So A Merry Christmas, uncle!"

"Good afternoon!" said Scrooge.

"And A Happy New Year!"

"Good afternoon!" said Scrooge.

His nephew left the room without an angry word, notwithstanding. He stopped at the outer door to bestow the greeting of the season on the clerk, who, cold as he was, was warmer than Scrooge; for he returned them cordially.

"There's another fellow," muttered Scrooge; who overheard him: "my clerk, custodian of a wife and young family, talking about a merry Christmas. The world is intent on mockery."

As Fred let himself out, he kindly let two gentlemen in. They were portly gentlemen, pleasant to behold, and now stood, with their hats off, in Scrooge's office. They had books and papers in their hands, and bowed to him.

"Scrooge and Marley's, I believe," said one of the gentlemen, referring to his list. "Have I the pleasure of addressing Mr Scrooge, or Mr Marley?"

"Mr Marley has been dead these three years," Scrooge replied. "He died three years ago, this very night."

"We have no doubt his reasonableness is well represented by his surviving partner," said the gentleman, presenting his credentials.

It certainly was; for they had been two kindred spirits. At the ominous word "reasonableness", Scrooge frowned, and shook his head, and handed the credentials back. University trustees. Those who would normally assist in funding the projects of Mr Scrooge and the Late Mr Marley. However, the death of Mr Marley on a misadventure had led the school to withdraw most of their research funding.

"At this festive season of the year, Mr Scrooge," said the gentleman, taking up a pen, "we are often required to make our final decisions with regards the limited funds left available for the University. We note that, for the third consecutive year, you have approached the Board of Trustees with regard to funding an exploration of the depths of the South Pacific."

"That would be a fair summary," Scrooge grunted.

"As you are no doubt aware, many departments are in want of basic provisions."

"Are there no funds for my research?"

"Plenty of funds, sir" said the gentleman, laying down his pen. "But those funds are to be distributed only in the pursuit of legitimate academic research."

"You imply my research lacks legitimacy?" demanded Scrooge.

"Oh, no! Not at all," the second gentleman interrupted, apologetically, "We merely wish for, ah…a little further…information regarding your proposed research."

"The findings of my research will be published upon my return and not a moment before. I'm sure you understand the need for such secrecy. One's reputation often relies on an assumption which merely requires tangible evidence. I am quite confident that I can provide this once I have returned." Scrooge may have been quietly avoided, occasionally despised, but he had learnt from Mr Marley the best methods of diplomacy when dealing with trustees and grantors.

"The Board have concerns," the first gentleman states, "that funding will be used to further your outlandish pursuit of the mythical city of R'lyeh. If this assumption is correct, sir, then we cannot grant you the funding you require."

"And why not?"

"Because the Miskatonic University will not fund any more damned crusades that Jacob Marley has brainwashed you in to pursuing." Gone now was any semblance of tact. The second gentleman now seemed intent on speaking ill of Scrooge's partner, which infuriated him.

"How dare you speak in such a way of Mr Marley, sir," Scrooge raged, "on this night of all nights!"

"Mr Marley was a lunatic and a suicide." The first gentleman's summary was spoken on behalf of the entire campus, Scrooge was sure of that much.

"Mr Marley was a scientist and a scholar. His research in to the lost city of R'lyeh…"

"Was unfounded and based solely upon vague hopes of recovering his late wife. Mr Marley was unwell. And this University has indulged his legacy of work for long enough."

Scrooge was silent. The first gentleman attempted to console him. "My sincere apologies, sir. I realise this is a crushing blow. And to advise you of this on Christmas, was…"

"Christmas? A humbug to Christmas! And to you! Bah!" And with that, Scrooge chased the trustees from his office. He slammed the door and turned to his trusted clerk, who watched with a sympathetic eye.

"I'm sorry, Mr Scrooge. I know how important your field research was to you." Cratchit offered, by way of condolence.

"Enough of that, Cratchit. I will not continue to be patronised tonight. Let us retire." Cratchit sprung from his desk and began to dress for the weather. Scrooge watched him and, with a sigh, said "You'll want the whole day tomorrow, I presume?"

"Please, sir," said Cratchit. "If it's convenient."

"It is not convenient, sir. And it is not fair. How must I apply for outside funding when my clerk will not report for duty when expected?" Scrooge paused, perhaps subconsciously aware of his temperament. Cratchit was not on the Board of Trustees, after all. Scrooge relented. "Very well. Take the whole day. But be here all the earlier the next morning."

"I will, sir. Thank you, sir."

Cratchit paused before leaving. Scrooge watched him before asking, "Is there anything else, Cratchit?"

"There is one other thing, sir."

"Oh?" offered Scrooge, amused at the boldness of Bob Cratchit. Never before had his clerk offered to stay a moment longer than necessary to speak to his employer.

Cratchit stuttered, "As a volunteer for my Church, sir, a few of us are endeavouring to raise a fund to buy the Poor some meat and drink, and means of warmth. We choose this time, because it is a time, of all others, when Want is keenly felt, and Abundance rejoices. May I put you down for a contribution, sir?"

"You may not!" Scrooge replied. "I don't make merry myself at Christmas and since this University can ill afford to make me merry in my work, I can't afford to make idle people merry. I help to support plenty of establishments, none of them with a basis in false religions. Perhaps those who are badly off should decide on a more rational choice than an Almighty God. Those who neglected to fund my research had better watch those unfortunate souls flock to places of worship such as that for Dagon. Perhaps then they will see my work as more than folly."

"And turn their backs on Christianity? Many would rather die."

"Then they will decrease the surplus population. It is not my concern. The shrines of the Old Ones lay hidden, ready to be explored, yet I am denied the privilege. If more prayed to them, perhaps my research would be justified." Scrooge paused, calming his hysteria. "You must excuse me, sir. I mean no offence. I find it is hard enough for a man to understand one's own business without interfering in other's. As you know, mine occupies me constantly and can result in irrational behaviour. Good afternoon, Cratchit."

Seeing clearly that it would be useless to pursue his point, Cratchit withdrew. Scrooge resumed his labours for a time, whilst the fog and darkness thickened. The ancient tower of a church, whose gruff old bell was always peeping slyly down at Scrooge out of a gothic window in the wall, became invisible, and struck the hours and quarters in the clouds, with tremulous vibrations afterwards as if its teeth were chattering in its frozen head up there. The cold became intense. In the main street, at the corner of the court, some labourers were repairing the gas-pipes, and had lighted a great fire in a brazier, round which a party of ragged men and boys were gathered: warming their hands and winking their eyes before the blaze in rapture. The brightness of the shops where holly sprigs and berries crackled in the lamp-heat of the windows, made pale faces ruddy as they passed. Poulterers' and grocers' trades became a splendid joke: a glorious pageant, with which it was next to impossible to believe that such dull principles as bargain and sale had anything to do.

As you may tell, I write with some sympathy towards Ebenezer Scrooge. Whilst his attitude and general demeanour left a lot to be desired, his problems were deep rooted. The loss of his sister and partner haunted him. Both lost at Christmastime. The season taunted him endlessly. But his true torture had yet to begin.

Scrooge had remained at his office for several hours following the departure of his clerk, pawing at hand drawn maps of the South Pacific. Of photographs of ruins taken on an Antarctic expedition that pointed towards a place of reverence or residence for the Old Ones, the Elder Gods. Had Scrooge been a wealthier man, he would have spent his last penny in a heartbeat to ensure passage to such ruins as these. The nearest he had come to a place renowned for the worship of Old Ones was his journey to Devil's Reef, a malignant island far off the coast of Innsmouth. Three had set out to the Reef that day, now ten years gone. Only two had returned. And of what Marley claimed to witness, Scrooge could tell no man for fear they would lock him away in the highest tower of the lunatic asylum.

Waking from his reverie, Scrooge locked his office and left, taking his usual melancholy dinner in his usual melancholy tavern; and having read all the newspapers, and beguiled the rest of the evening with his maps and charts, went home to bed. He lived in chambers which had once belonged to his deceased partner. They were a gloomy suite of rooms, in a lowering pile of building behind the warehouses on River Street, where it had so little business to be, that one could scarcely help fancying it must have run there when it was a young house, playing at hide-and-seek with other houses, and have forgotten the way out again. It was decrepit and decaying now, a result of a constant battery of weather that flowed down the Miskatonic River. And it was quiet at night, for nobody lived in it but Scrooge, the other rooms being all let out as offices. The yard was so dark that even Scrooge, who knew its every stone, was fain to grope with his hands.

Now, it is a fact, that there was nothing at all particular about the knocker on the door, except that it was very large. It is also a fact, that Scrooge had seen it, night and morning, during his whole residence in that place; also that Scrooge had as little of what is called fancy about him as any man in Massachusetts. Let it also be borne in mind that Scrooge had not bestowed one thought on Marley, since leaving his office earlier that evening. This is expressly stated in Scrooge's journal and, as such, should be expressly stated here. Of what happened next, the University would have me censor. For the purposes of accuracy I will tell you exactly what Ebenezer Scrooge claimed he saw and invite you, the reader, to ascertain its credibility. However, I must warn you; this is but the first of a series of supernatural events to befall Scrooge on this night.

Scrooge tells that, having his key in the lock of the door, he saw in the knocker, without its undergoing any intermediate process of change: not a knocker, but Marley's face.

For those who may try to discount this as fancy, I will add that Marley's face was not as Scrooge would remember it. It was bluing, bloated and showing signs of rot. Water dripped from his chin, be that of precipitous origin or some other ghastly place, I cannot say. His lips were peeling and chapped – not as lips may be from the cold, but as if they had been chewed or nibbled by small fry. The mouth was contorted in to a grimace. Not angry or ferocious, but frozen in agony and suffering. As if his face had borne a tremendous suffering for this past three years.

Scrooge, having immediately taken a step back, moved in closer. Convinced of the falsity of the apparition, Scrooge reached out and touched Marley's cold, clammy cheek. As his fingers touched that rigid, dead skin, Marley's eyes jolted open. They were milky. The lack of pupils gave him a startled look, which made Scrooge's stomach wretch. The hair was curiously stirred, as if underwater; and, though the eyes were wide open, they were perfectly motionless. That, and its livid colour, made it horrible; but its horror seemed to be in spite of the face and beyond its control, rather than a part of its own expression.

In that long, terrified moment, Scrooge watched as Marley opened his mouth. His jaw extended unnaturally and his glassy eyes bore in to Scrooge's soul as he cried; "Scrooge!"

Scrooge covered his face in horror, hoping to shut out whatever ghastly scenes would play out from henceforth. But there was silence. He peered out from behind his hands and Marley was gone. The knocker stood lifeless; it was a knocker again.

To say that he was not startled, or that his blood was not conscious of a terrible sensation to which it had been a stranger from infancy, would be untrue. But he put his hand upon the key he had relinquished, turned it sturdily and walked in.

He did pause, with a moment's irresolution, before he shut the door; and he did look cautiously behind it first, as if he half expected to be terrified with the sight of

Marley's pigtail sticking out into the hall. But there was nothing on the back of the door, except the screws and nuts that held the knocker on. With a muttered "Humbug!" Scrooge slammed the door.

The sound resounded through the house like thunder. Every room above, and every cask in the wine-merchant's cellars below, appeared to have a separate peal of echoes of its own. Scrooge was not a man to be frightened by echoes. He fastened the door, and walked across the hall, and up the stairs, slowly too. But before he shut his heavy door, he walked through his rooms to see that all was right. He had just enough recollection of the face to desire to do that.

As you may assume, he found them all as they should be. Whether you believe Scrooge's account or you consider it an advanced hallucination, he was perfectly reasoned in examining his quarters before he relaxed. Nobody under the table, nobody under the sofa. Nobody under the bed; nobody in the closet; nobody in his dressing-gown, which was hanging up in a suspicious attitude against the wall. Lumber-room as usual. Old fire-guard, old shoes, two fish-baskets, washing-stand on three legs, and a poker. Having reassured himself, Scrooge set about preparing a small glass of whisky, then double locked his door, which was not his custom. In retrospect, had Scrooge done the right thing? For although he had secured himself (or so he thought) from those outside, he had also prevented his escape should there be someone (or something) in the apartment with him.

Scrooge settled in front of his fireplace, journal in hand. The fireplace was an old one, built by some Dutch merchant who had briefly stayed in Arkham whilst working in the warehouses a number of years ago. It was paved all round with quaint Dutch tiles, designed to illustrate the Scriptures. There were Cains and Abels, Pharaoh's daughters, Queens of Sheba, Angelic messengers descending through the air on clouds like feather-beds, Abrahams, Belshazzars, Apostles putting off to sea in butter-boats. No Old Ones, which had always amused Marley. What with the establishment of the Esoteric Order of Dagon in nearby Innsmouth in recent years, it seemed remiss not to include them in illustrations of messengers descending from the skies and beings emerging from beneath the waves. He sat staring at the hundreds of figures to attract his thoughts; and yet that face of Marley, three years dead, came and swallowed up the whole. If each smooth tile had been a blank at first, with power to shape some picture on its surface from the disjointed fragments of his thoughts, there would have been a copy of old Marley's head on every one. Scrooge stared at a tile depicting a seaward journey of Apostles. There appeared to be lettering carved in to the side of their boats that Scrooge had never noticed before. He read it out loud to himself.

"Cthulhu fhtagn..." repeated Scrooge; and walked across the room to his bookshelf, pulling down a book of Marley's scrawlings.

He sat back down in his chair and leafed through pages of musings on the Elder Gods, of the myth of Cthulhu and the Deep Ones, of Dagon and Hydra. His eyes grew heavy as he studied and his head fell back in the chair. As he began to slumber, he heard a light tapping coming from his window. The tapping slowly developed in to a rattle, which Scrooge attributed to the wind blowing through the gaps in the nearby warehouses. That was until a thought dawned on him. With horror, he recalled no breeze on his walk home from the University. There could be no wind. Something was knocking, now louder and harder than before, banging at his window to get in. He jumped up and his eyes darted to the window, just in time for the banging to cease and just in time for a last glimpse of something long and slimy. The culprit of the knocking. From his semi-slumber, it resembled a tentacle, but his glimpse was far too brief to establish a clear identity. It is a recollection such as this that lends such weighty credence to Mr Scrooge's account of events. If the entire story was a flight of fancy, why not elaborate on what he saw tapping at his window?

Now wide awake and shaking with adrenaline, Scrooge rushed to the window in hopes of catching a clearer look at his mystery knocker. But there was nothing. He craned his neck to glimpse down the alleyway towards the River. He was suddenly aware of the washing of the water against the riverbank. There was a ripple, barely discernible in the moonlight but Scrooge's senses were heightened to a state of maximum alert. The ripple gave rise to a hand, which clawed its way out of the river, dragging a near lifeless body behind it. Scrooge immediately presumed some poor soul had rescued himself from drowning. Perhaps some idle Christmas merrymaker had fallen in to the river whilst inebriated. But the drowned body – for he could not be called a living person – drew itself to its feet, glassy eyes glowing in the moonlight as it stared up at Scrooge's window. Feeling suddenly exposed, Scrooge quickly drew the curtains closed and held them there, gasping in horror.

He waited. Merely a few minutes, but an eternity to his thumping heart, before slowly peeling the curtains open a crack and slowly peering out. What he saw was a great, dead eye staring back through the window from his fourth storey window ledge. The creature, through some means unnatural, had climbed to his window and now pressed wet hands against the glass, as if ready to reach in and pull Scrooge out.

Scrooge closed the curtains in a vain attempt to block out the horror and staggered away from the window, his breath catching in his throat. "It's humbug still! I won't believe it!" Scrooge cried as he stood listening to the windows crack under the pressure of the hands pressed against them. The creaked and snapped and with a great crash exploded. The curtains flew from the rails as a torrent of water came pouring in through the open window, as if a hull had been breached on a seafaring vessel. Scrooge tried to shield himself from the blast, but the tsunami engulfed him and he was drowned. As the water slowly began to dissipate, Scrooge wiped his eyes. The rushing of the water in his ears had ceased and he stared in horror at what stood before him.

As I have stated, Scrooge's account up until this point can be dismissed as dream or fever. Let it be known that, in examining Scrooge's apartment after the fact, the window was still intact. Whether it had been replaced or had never been breached, I cannot say. But the carpets and walls were consistent with significant water damage that would suggest a great deal of flooding. Let us therefore assume that what Scrooge describes was indeed what happened. And let us therefore assume that the thing that stood before him was also as Scrooge describes. And the description matches that of Scrooge's doorknocker.

The same face: the very same. Marley in his pigtail, wringing with sea water, his clothes – waistcoat, trousers, shirt and boots – dripping wet from his emergence on to land. His face was so pale and bloated as to give a transparent effect, with Scrooge observing his dead veins and musculature beneath his stretched skin.

Scrooge could scarcely believe it. There before him stood Marley. A phantom, of sorts. Clammy and cold, like a corpse, but stood before him all the same. He looked the phantom through and through, and saw it standing before him, silent; though he felt the chilling influence of its death-cold eyes; and marked the very texture of the folded kerchief bound about its head and chin, which wrapper he had not observed before; he was still incredulous, and fought against his senses.

"How now!" said Scrooge, caustic and cold as ever. "What do you want with me?"

"Much!" -- Marley's voice, no doubt about it. Oh, how Scrooge had missed Marley's voice.

"Who are you?" It can be said that even when provided with absolute proof, the phantom of his dead partner stood before him, Scrooge still questioned. It seemed such an illogical question once he had asked it.

"Ask me who I was."

"Who were you then." said Scrooge, raising his voice. "You're particular, for a shade." And with that, Scrooge did not require further proof, for Marley was as particular a man as any Scrooge had met.

"In life I was your partner, Jacob Marley."

"Can you -- can you sit down?" asked Scrooge, looking doubtfully at him.

"I can."

"Do it, then."

Scrooge asked the question, because he was unsure whether the figure of Marley was a spectre or some form of living dead. And if Marley's body was tangible, it looked set to burst on contact, a bubble of noxious gases and decayed organs. But Marley sat down on the opposite side of the fireplace, as if he were quite used to it.

"You don't believe in me," observed the Ghost.

"I don't," said Scrooge.

"What evidence would you have of my reality beyond that of your senses?"

"I don't know," said Scrooge.

"Why do you doubt your senses?"

"Because," said Scrooge, "a little thing affects them. A slight disorder of the stomach makes them cheats. You may be an undigested bit of beef, a blot of mustard, a crumb of cheese, a fragment of an underdone potato. There's more of gravy than of grave about you, whatever you are!"

Scrooge was not much in the habit of cracking jokes, not since Marley had last departed. It was quite possible that he had resorted to humour as a means of relief. Did Scrooge feel satiated by the return of his partner? For surely Marley's return meant there was still hope for Scrooge's dear sister, Fan. The truth is, that he tried to be smart, as a means of distracting his own attention, and keeping down his terror; for the spectre's voice disturbed the very marrow in his bones.

To sit, staring at those fixed, glazed eyes, in silence for a moment, would play, Scrooge felt, the very deuce with him. There was something very awful, too, as if the Being identified as Marley provided an infernal atmosphere all of its own. Scrooge could not feel it himself, but observed as much for his journal; for though the Being sat perfectly motionless, its hair, and shirt, and waistcoat, were still agitated as if it were still being drawn down in to the endless depths of the ocean.

"You see this toothpick?" said Scrooge, returning quickly to the charge, for the reason just assigned; and wishing, though it were only for a second, to divert the vision's stony gaze from himself.

"I do," replied the Being.

"You are not looking at it," said Scrooge, frustratedly.

"But I see it," said the Being, "notwithstanding."

"Well!" returned Scrooge, "I have but to swallow this, and be for the rest of my days persecuted by a legion of goblins, all of my own creation. Humbug, I tell you; humbug!"

At this the spirit raised a frightful cry, "Ph'nglui mglw'nafh Cthulhu R'lyeh wgah'nagl fhtagn!" Scrooge held on tight to his chair, to save himself from falling in a swoon. But his horror would grow greater. The Being that called itself Marley, reached around the top of its head and tore off the bandage it wore. Its lower jaw dropped down to its breast and it screamed before projecting a stream of rancid seawater out on to the floor. Scrooge recoiled in horror and the Being gripped its jaw and lifted it back in to position with a crack.

Scrooge fell upon his knees, and clasped his hands before his face.

"Mercy!" he said. "Dreadful monstrosity, why do you trouble me?"

"Man of the worldly mind!" replied the Being, "do you believe in me or not?"

"I do," said Scrooge. "I must. But why do spirits walk the earth, and why do they come to me?"

"You consider me a spirit?" Marley questioned, "Why?"

"Are you not a spirit?"

"You forget our research, Ebenezer. You forget our search for R'lyeh, for Dagon and Hydra. Do you so quickly forget the face of your beloved sister, now ten years passed?"

"I don't forget! I won't forget!" Scrooge pleaded.

"It is required every Christmas," Marley returned, "that the Elder Ones walk abroad among humankind, and travel far and wide in search of a sacrifice. A sacrifice for the Great Cthulhu, so that he may yet sleep for another year unfettered. So this has continued for aeons and so it must continue this night. And should the Elder Ones identify one of the Elder bloodline, he will be pursued, for Cthulhu craves those who have hybrid blood in their veins. Such a man is doomed." Again the spectre raised a cry, and vomited a projectile spray of seawater. As his jaw hung open, Scrooge observed large slits on the side of his neck.

"Gills, Marley?" said Scrooge, trembling. "Tell me why?"

"I wear the mark of mixed blood. The result of cross species breeding. I made myself a sacrifice to Dagon and am slowly taken with the Innsmouth Look."

"The Innsmouth Look?" Scrooge recalled Marley's notebook, now abandoned on the arm of the chair. "The result of mating between humans and Deep Ones? Surely the legends cannot be true."

"Did you ever doubt them, Scrooge? My transformation is not yet complete. When it is so, I will join my brethren in Y'ha-nthlei and I will never return to the surface." Scrooge observed a sorrow in Marley's voice. Whilst the mixing of human and Deep One blood would undoubtedly make Marley immortal, Marley would no longer be welcome on the surface. Not until the undersea cities rose again - Y'ha-nthlei and R'lyeh – and with them, the slumbering Elders. *Cthulhu fhtagn*.

Despite this, Scrooge could not help but feel a twinge of excitement. The opportunity to explore the lost undercities of the Old Ones was too tempting for Old Ebenezer. But his excitement did not last long. His mind turned back to his original goal, the reason he had pursued the underwater cities. Fan.

"What of Fan, Jacob? What of my sister?"

"All is as I thought ten years previous, Ebenezer," Marley replied. "Fan was recovered from the shipwreck by Deep Ones who dwelt upon Devil's Reef. They nursed her, but her wounds were too deep. They started the transformation to save her life. Fan is now fully transformed. She barely remembers her life as a human. She would not remember you."

Scrooge choked. His sister had survived. Moreso, she was now immortal and dwelling with Deep Ones. Scrooge steadied himself against a chair, uncertain of how much more he could fathom. "I must go to her. I must see her." Scrooge demanded, but Marley did not move.

"Your fate is not that of your sister. Nor is it my fate. You have sought the Great Cthulhu and now, in return, Cthulhu seeks you. You are to be the sacrifice, Scrooge. Through your suffering, the Elder Things will bestow pleasant dreams upon the people of the Earth, that which Christianity may refer to as Christmas cheer."

"Jacob," Scrooge said, imploringly. "Old Jacob Marley, tell me more. Speak comfort to me, Jacob."

"I have none to give," Marley replied. "It comes from other regions, Ebenezer Scrooge, and is conveyed by other ministers, to other kinds of men. I have conveyed all that the Deep Ones will permit me to say. I cannot rest, I cannot stay, I cannot linger anywhere. My spirit never walked beyond our offices -- mark me! -- in life I may have sought adventure and exploration, but my spirit never roved beyond the narrow limits of our poorly-funded hole; now weary journeys lie before me before the day that I crawl in to the sea, never to re-emerge."

"Three years gone," mused Scrooge. "And travelling all the time?"

"The whole time," said the Deep One.

"You travel fast?" said Scrooge.

"On the pulling of the tide," replied Marley.

"You might have got over a great quantity of exploration in three years," said Scrooge. "Places and hidden relics the likes of which I can only imagine. What wonders, Marley!"

The Being, on hearing this, set up another cry, and more sea water poured forth from its terrible gaping mouth, its gills held wide drawing air in to the lifeless lungs.

"Oh! Captive and bound to the will of Elder Things," cried Marley, "not to know, that ages of incessant labour by immortal creatures, for this earth must pass into eternity before the good of which it is susceptible is all developed. Not to know that any human spirit working kindly in its little sphere, whatever it may be, will find its mortal life too short for its vast means of usefulness. Not to know that no space of regret can make amends for one life's opportunities misused! Yet such was I! Oh! such was I!"

"But you were a good scholar, Jacob," faltered Scrooge, who now began to apply this to himself.

"Scholar!" cried the Being, wringing its hands again. "Such would be true if I were a scholar of humankind. Charitable, merciful, benevolent. Would I were as good a husband had I been a scholar. Perhaps then I would not have encouraged my wife to attend an expedition that resulted in her loss. Never should I have sought the infernal creatures that we have now become. Undying, but forever dead. Forever to dwell in the shadow of the Great Cthulhu, praying for the day we can roam freely upon the surface of our planet."

It held its hands up to its gills and nursed them, solemnly.

"At this time of the year," it said, "I suffer most. Why did I walk through crowds of fellow-beings with my eyes turned down, only raising them to wonder at the Beings that dwelled in the heavens above us? Were there no poor homes to which the light of those stars could have conducted me!"

Scrooge was very much dismayed to hear his partner going on at this rate, and began to quake exceedingly.

"Hear me!" cried the Deep One. "My time is nearly gone."

"I will," said Scrooge. "But don't be hard upon me, Jacob! Pray!"

"I surface tonight as part of my penance," pursued Marley. "I am here tonight to warn you, that you have yet a chance and hope of escaping my fate. A chance and hope of my procuring, Ebenezer."

"You were always a good friend to me," said Scrooge. "Thank'ee!"

"You will be visited," resumed Marley, "by Three Elders."

Scrooge's countenance fell almost as low as his partner's had done.

"Is that the chance and hope you mentioned, Jacob?" he demanded, in a faltering voice.

"It is."

"I -- I think I'd rather not," said Scrooge.

"Without their visits," said the Ghost, "you cannot hope to escape your sacrifice to the Great Cthulhu. Expect the first tonight, when the bell tolls One."

"Couldn't I take them all at once, and have it over, Jacob?" asked Scrooge.

"Expect the second when the bell tolls Two. The third upon the next hour, when the bell tolls Three. Look to see me no more; and look that, for your own sake, you remember what has passed between us."

When it had said these words, the being took its wrapper from the table, and bound it round its head, as before. Scrooge knew this, by the smart sound its teeth made, when the jaws were brought together by the bandage. He ventured to raise his eyes again, and found his supernatural visitor confronting him in an erect attitude, its damp clothes stained by seaweed.

The figure of Jacob Marley stood perfectly still next to the smashed window. Scrooge felt a tremor and stepped back as the puddles of water scattered about the room began to quake. Suddenly, the water lifted from the floor and walls, forming droplets that swarmed around the room in a circular fashion. Scrooge shrank in to the corner to avoid being caught in the veritable whirlpool erupting in his room. As the water spun faster, Scrooge shielded his eyes. He heard the sound of distant thunder and he opened his eyes to find his room deserted, the window intact but wide open and rain pelting through the open window as a storm thundered outside.

Scrooge rushed to the window to close it, presuming some foul nightmare or fever had taken him. He glanced out towards the river and saw them.

Not so much in obedience, as in surprise and fear: for on the raising of the hand, he became sensible of confused noises in the air; incoherent sounds of lamentation and regret; wailings inexpressibly sorrowful and self-accusatory. The spectre, after listening for a moment, joined in the mournful dirge; and floated out upon the bleak, dark night.

Scrooge followed to the window: desperate in his curiosity. He looked out.

The air was filled with lights, wandering hither and thither in restless haste. It is possible that this may have been a trick of the light in the sudden thunderstorm, or perhaps a sighting of Aurora Borealis. Yet Scrooge knew them to be Outer Gods. He watched as they circled each other far in outer space, piping demong flutes and dancing to the whim of Azathoth. They were restless this Christmas Eve. They required sacrifice and Jacob Marley had made their intentions clear. They would come for Ebenezer Scrooge. They would seek to show him vile, unspeakable horrors designed to warp his mind in to accepting his fate as the Christmas sacrifice to Cthulhu. Perhaps the research of Scrooge and Marley had angered the Gods? It is now impossible to say, but we can be assured of their all-seeing, all-knowing nature as a result of what has happened to Scrooge – in events so far transcribed and what transpired following his ghastly encounter.

Turning to the river, Scrooge saw Old Marley slowly wading back out in to the water. As he did so, the water rippled and convulsed and there rose at least ten of Marley's fellow creatures. Their faces were difficult to make out in the storm, but their skin was dark grey, most no longer wore clothes. They stood upon the banks of the river, slimy monstrosities from another world, bizarre hybrids of man and gods. Each of them stared as Marley had at his window and watched him and Scrooge thought he could hear the sound of laughter. The delight of the Deep Ones as they howled and mocked at one who was cursed to die. He held back a whimper as he thrust his head back inside the room, slamming the window closed behind him.

Suddenly, the thunderstorm stopped, the echoes of the laughter were gone. The window showed no sign of tampering or breaking as it had earlier in the night. Had Scrooge been taken to fancy? I can assure you, he had not. But, for the moment at least, Scrooge felt safe and secure at home. All had been as it was before his journey home from the University. There were no phantom doorknockers, no Outer Gods or Deep Ones. Marley's notebook remained on the arm of the chair. Scrooge examined it. Bone dry. A dream for certain then. He replaced it on the bookshelf and thought no more of Jacob Marley, his sister or exploration of underwater cities, for he feared a fever had come upon him and was projecting his thoughts and wishes in to vivid dreams.

He tried to say "Humbug!" but stopped at the first syllable. And being, from the emotion he had undergone, or the fatigues of the day, or his glimpse of the Outer Gods in their heavenly world, or the dull conversation of the remnants of Jacob Marley, or the lateness of the hour, much in need of repose; went straight to bed, without undressing, wrote a frantic journal entry – the contents of which I have now described for you, and fell asleep. Would that his night be undisturbed, buut the worst horrors were yet to come for poor Old Ebenezer.

II

So it was that Scrooge slept, not a fanciful sleep filled with dreams – for dreams can be gateways to the living realms of the Gods – but an uneventful, if restless sleep. His mind could not help but wander to his sister, Fan, taken from him ten years ago. He raged of his vision earlier that night, of an imagined conversation with Jacob Marley and a chance of procuring his sister once again. It all seemed so cruel, to have one's sister presented yet again and have her snatched away so suddenly. He made a note never to eat at the restaurant near the University again, presuming his vivid waking nightmares to be a result of some stale food.

Of this portion of events, I relate to you from a mixture of journal and conversation. Scrooge kept his journal on him at all times, including at night, for he would often wake to note down some half remembered dream before it faded from memory. Both Scrooge and Marley theorised that dreams were memories of forgotten worlds and consciousness. They considered them to be of vital importance in establishing contact with lost cities such as R'lyeh. It will become clear in my account that Scrooge was incapable of noting every last detail of what occurred and of this I will expand based upon conversations I have had with Ebenezer Scrooge in recent days.

Miskatonic University would consider such a statement to be lunacy, but I invite the reader to draw their own conclusions as to the validity of my musings.

What of Scrooge that night? Was he visited by Gods, intent on proving his worth as a festive sacrifice? When Scrooge awoke, it was so dark, that looking out of bed, he could scarcely distinguish the transparent window from the opaque walls of his chamber. He was endeavouring to pierce the darkness with his ferret eyes, when the chimes of a neighbouring church struck the four quarters. So he listened for the hour.

To his great astonishment the heavy bell went on from six to seven, and from seven to eight, and regularly up to twelve; then stopped. Twelve! It was past two when he went to bed. The clock was wrong. An icicle must have got into the works. Twelve! He touched the spring of his repeater, to correct this most preposterous clock. Its rapid little pulse beat twelve: and stopped. `Why, it isn't possible, thought Scrooge, `that I can have slept through a whole day and far into another night? It isn't possible that anything has happened to the sun, and this is twelve at noon! Was he dreaming? Had he passed in to another realm? Was this Lomar, location of the famed Pnakotic Manuscripts – an arcane tome that predates man and tells of the history of the Elder Gods? Scrooge had read of occurrences in which people visited Lomar in their dreams, as vivid as real life. More than one man had been committed for believing Lomar to be real and our world to be a dream from which they could not awaken. Was Scrooge now on the brink of insanity, also?

The idea being an alarming one, he scrambled out of bed, and groped his way to the window. He was obliged to rub the frost off with the sleeve of his dressing-gown before he could see anything; and could see very little then. All he could make out was, that it was still very foggy and extremely cold, and that there was no noise of people running to and fro, and making a great stir, as there unquestionably would have been if night had beaten off bright day, and taken possession of the world. Nor was the city of Lomar beyond his window, which filled him with a great relief. There stood the great warehouses of River Street and beyond that the Miskatonic, silent and dark.

Scrooge went to bed again, and thought, and thought, and thought it over and over, and could make nothing of it. The more he thought, the more perplexed he was; and the more he endeavoured not to think, the more he thought, Marley's visit bothered him exceedingly. Every time he resolved within himself, after mature inquiry, that it was all a dream, his mind flew back, like a strong spring released, to its first position, and presented the same problem to be worked all through, Was it a dream or not? And if not, what of the time difference now? Was it merely coincidence that both the church clock and his own clock had malfunctioned at the same time?

Scrooge lay in this state until the chime had gone three quarters more, when he remembered, on a sudden, that Marley had warned him of a visitation when the bell tolled one. He resolved to lie awake until the hour was past; and, considering that he could no more go to sleep than go to Heaven, this was perhaps the wisest resolution in his power. He would, at the very least, prove his madness to himself and be content with it. Content enough to sleep, at any rate. On Christmas morning he would endeavour to obtain a full diagnosis.

The quarter was so long, that he was more than once convinced he must have sunk into a doze unconsciously, and missed the clock. At length it broke upon his listening ear.

"Ding, dong!"

"A quarter past," Scrooge counted.

"Ding, dong!"

"Half past!" said Scrooge.

"Ding, dong!"

"A quarter to it," said Scrooge.

"Ding, dong!"

The hour itself, and nothing more. He was truly mad, and for that he was relieved. He let out one long laugh, but it was far too soon, for he had spoke before the hour bell sounded, which it now did with a deep, dull, hollow, melancholy ONE. Light flashed up in the room upon the instant, and the curtains of his bed were drawn.

I had asked Scrooge if he had jumped out of bed of his own accord, but he was most insistent on the following point; the curtains of his bed were drawn aside by a hand. Not the curtains at his feet, nor the curtains at his back, but those to which his face was addressed. The curtains of his bed were drawn aside; and Scrooge, starting up into a half-recumbent attitude, found himself face to face with the unearthly visitor who drew them: as close to it as this page is to your eyes. As the words I write watch you, so did the ghostly figure before Scrooge, who trembled. After the horrors of Jacob Marley and the Deep Ones earlier that night, Scrooge averted his eyes from the creature. What manner of horror could be stood before him? Some hideous, dripping beast from another world, waiting to feast on his mortal flesh? Scrooge peered through his fingers at his unwelcome visitor. The figure before him was not what was expected, but may as well have been, considering Scrooge's fear.

It was a strange figure -- like a child: yet not so like a child as like an old man, viewed through some supernatural medium, which gave him the appearance of having receded from the view, and being diminished to a child's proportions. Its hair, which hung about its neck and down its back, was white as if with age; and yet the face had not a wrinkle in it, and the tenderest bloom was on the skin. The arms were very long and muscular; the hands the same, as if its hold were of uncommon strength. Its legs and feet, most delicately formed, were, like those upper members, bare. It wore a tunic of the purest white and round its waist was bound a lustrous belt, the sheen of which was beautiful. It held a branch of fresh green holly in its hand; and, in singular contradiction of that wintry emblem, had its dress trimmed with summer flowers. But the strangest thing about it was, that from the crown of its head there sprung a bright clear jet of light, by which all this was visible; and which was doubtless the occasion of its using, in its duller moments, a great extinguisher for a cap, which it now held under its arm.

Even this, though, when Scrooge looked at it with increasing steadiness, was not its strangest quality. For as its belt sparkled and glittered now in one part and now in another, and what was light one instant, at another time was dark, so the figure itself fluctuated in its distinctness: being now a thing with one arm, now with one leg, now with twenty legs, now a pair of legs without a head, now a head without a body: of which dissolving parts, no outline would be visible in the dense gloom wherein they melted away. And in the very wonder of this, it would be itself again; distinct and clear as ever.

"Are you the Spirit, sir, whose coming was foretold to me?" asked Scrooge.

"I am," the figure stated. Was this one of the Elder race of Gods? For it seemed to Scrooge much more like an apparition. The voice was soft and gentle. Singularly low, as if instead of being so close beside him, it were at a distance.

"Who, and what are you?" Scrooge demanded.

"I fell from outside the ordered universe. From that amorphous blight of nethermost confusion which blasphemes and bubbles at the center of all infinity, from the boundless daemon sultan Azathoth, whose name no lips dare speak aloud, and who gnaws hungrily in inconceivable, unlighted chambers beyond time and space amidst the muffled, maddening beating of vile drums and the thin monotonous whine of accursed flutes," The bizarre phantom spoke.

"You fell?" Scrooge asked.

"From the service of the noxious Azathoth, who bubbles and blasphemes at the centre of All Things, to the servitude of Betelgeuse."

Scrooge understood, for the manuscripts told that the Elder Gods ruled from Betelgeuse and fought the Great Old Ones, led by Azathoth – the blind idiot god. Was this what he had seen from his window? Had the Great Old Ones amassed in the nearby stars, in search of this fallen god? Or were they watching, mockingly as the Elder Gods failed to rise at their expected hour of Christmas? Any theory I relate to you at this point would merely be conjecture.

"By what may I address you?" offered Scrooge.

The phantom appeared to pause, considering, then replied, "I am the Ghost of Christmas Past."

"Long past?" inquired Scrooge, "Of the days before man, the city of Lomar, the slumber of the Elder Gods?"

"No. Your past."

The light streaming forth from this Old One was blinding and haunting, and Scrooge could take no more. With trembling voice, he asked the phantom to cover itself with its cap.

"What!" exclaimed the Ghost, "would you so soon put out, with worldly hands, the light I give? Is it not enough that you are one of those whose passions made this cap, and force me through whole trains of years to wear it low upon my brow? How can this pitiful race of mortals ever transcend when enlightenment is shunned by so many."

Scrooge reverently disclaimed all intention to offend or any knowledge of having wilfully bonneted the Spirit at any period of his life. He then made bold to inquire what business brought him there.

"Your welfare, for better or worse. You must decide," said the Ghost.

Scrooge expressed himself much obliged, but could not help thinking that a night of unbroken rest would have been more conducive to that end. The Spirit must have heard him thinking, for it said immediately:

"Your reclamation, then. Take heed!"

It put out its strong hand as it spoke, and clasped him gently by the arm.

"Rise and walk with me."

It would have been in vain for Scrooge to plead that the weather and the hour were not adapted to pedestrian purposes; that bed was warm, and the thermometer a long way below freezing; that he was clad but lightly in his slippers, dressing-gown, and nightcap; and that he had a cold upon him at that time. The grasp, though gentle as a woman's hand, was not to be resisted. He rose: but finding that the Spirit made towards the window, clasped his robe in supplication.

"I am mortal," Scrooge remonstrated, "and liable to fall."

"Bear but a touch of my hand there," said the Spirit, laying it upon his heart, "and you shall be upheld in more than this!"

As the words were spoken, they passed through the wall, and stood upon an open country road, with fields on either hand. The city had entirely vanished. Not a vestige of it was to be seen. The darkness and the mist had vanished with it, for it was a clear, cold, winter day, with snow upon the ground. "Good Heaven!" said Scrooge, clasping his hands together, as he looked about him. "I was bred in this place. I was a boy here!"

The Spirit gazed upon him mildly. Its gentle touch, though it had been light and instantaneous, appeared still present to the old man's sense of feeling. He was conscious of a thousand odours floating in the air, each one connected with a thousand thoughts, and hopes, and joys, and cares long, long, forgotten.

"Your lip is trembling," said the Ghost. "And what is that upon your cheek?"

Scrooge muttered, with an unusual catching in his voice, that it was a pimple; and begged the Ghost to lead him where he would.

"You recollect the way?" inquired the Spirit.

"Remember it!" cried Scrooge with fervour; "I could walk it blindfold."

"Strange to have forgotten it for so many years!" observed the Ghost.

"I had not forgotten," Scrooge said, "It is some distance to travel. I work in the city. The country is of little importance now."

"This small township in which you grew lies outside of Innsmouth, does it not?" the phantom asked.

"Some ways, yes," Scrooge answered.

"By train?"

"Less than a day's journey, I imagine."

"And three years ago, you could not make such a small journey to bid farewell to your partner, Mr Marley?" the Ghost asked, "He was laid to rest at Innsmouth, or so you thought, was he not?"

"Overlooking the harbour," Scrooge replied. An empty grave in Marley's home town, the residents unaware that Marley survived, transformed, and dwelt in the immeasurable fathoms below.

They walked along the road; Scrooge recognising every gate, and post, and tree; until a little market-town appeared in the distance, with its bridge, its church, and winding river. Some shaggy ponies now were seen trotting towards them with boys upon their backs, who called to other boys in country gigs and carts, driven by farmers. All these boys were in great spirits, and shouted to each other, until the broad fields were so full of merry music, that the crisp air laughed to hear it.

"Will they not fear the sight of a Great Old One?" Scrooge asked, conscious that they both stood upon the road.

"These are but shadows of the things that have been," said the Ghost. "They have no consciousness of us."

The jocund travellers came on; and as they came, Scrooge knew and named them every one. Why was he rejoiced beyond all bounds to see them? Why did his cold eye glisten, and his heart leap up as they went past? Why was he filled with gladness when he heard them give each other Merry Christmas, as they parted at cross-roads and bye-ways, for their several homes? What was merry Christmas to Scrooge? Out upon merry Christmas! What good had it ever done to him?

"The school is not quite deserted," said the Ghost. "A solitary child, neglected by his friends, is left there still."

Scrooge said he knew it. And he sobbed.

They left the high-road, by a well-remembered lane, and soon approached a mansion of dull red brick, with a little weathercock-surmounted cupola, on the roof, and a bell hanging in it. It was a large house, but one of broken fortunes; for the spacious offices were little used, their walls were damp and mossy, their windows broken, and their gates decayed. Fowls clucked and strutted in the stables; and the coach-houses and sheds were over-run with grass. Nor was it more retentive of its ancient state, within; for entering the dreary hall, and glancing through the open doors of many rooms, they found them poorly furnished, cold, and vast. There was an earthy savour in the air, a chilly bareness in the place, which associated itself somehow with too much getting up by candle-light, and not too much to eat.

They went, the Ghost and Scrooge, across the hall, to a door at the back of the house. It opened before them, and disclosed a long, bare, melancholy room, made barer still by lines of plain deal forms and desks. At one of these a lonely boy was reading near a feeble fire; and Scrooge sat down upon a form, and wept to see his poor forgotten self as he used to be. Not a latent echo in the house, not a squeak and scuffle from the mice behind the panelling, not a drip from the half-thawed water-spout in the dull yard behind, not a sigh among the leafless boughs of one despondent poplar, not the idle swinging of an empty store-house door, no, not a clicking in the fire, but fell upon the heart of Scrooge with a softening influence, and gave a freer passage to his tears.

The Spirit touched him on the arm, and pointed to his younger self, intent upon his reading.

"Why show me these things, Spirit?" Scrooge commanded. "Marley told me that the Elders sought to bring festive cheer to mortals, yet never has this cheer fallen upon me. Look! Alone, abandoned, why show me this?"

"It is the beginning of things. Of events that would lead you to your present situation. Take heed, Scrooge, for although your Christmases may not have been merry, they were once happy. Long before your research, mind."

"I wish," Scrooge muttered, putting his hand in his pocket, and looking about him, after drying his eyes with his cuff: "but it's too late now."

"What is the matter?" asked the Spirit.

"Nothing," said Scrooge. "Nothing. You speak of a time before I began my research into long forgotten history. If only I had abandoned such lines of study and not gotten caught up in myths and legends as a young boy. Perhaps then, I could have saved her."

"You speak of your sister?" The Ghost asked.

"Always so indulgent of me," Scrooge recalled, "Always so encouraging, even unto her death."

The Ghost smiled thoughtfully, and waved its hand: saying as it did so, "Let us see another Christmas!"

Scrooge's former self grew larger at the words, and the room became a little darker and dirtier. The panels shrunk, the windows cracked; fragments of plaster fell out of the ceiling, and the naked laths were shown instead; but how all this was brought about, Scrooge could no more say than I. He only knew that it was quite correct; that everything had happened so; that there he was, alone again, when all the other boys had gone home for the holidays.

He was not reading now, but walking up and down despairingly. Scrooge looked at the Ghost, and with a mournful shaking of his head, glanced anxiously towards the door.

It opened; and a little girl, much younger than the boy, came darting in, and putting her arms about his neck, and often kissing him, addressed him as her "Dear, dear brother."

"I have come to bring you home, dear brother!" said the child, clapping her tiny hands, and bending down to laugh. "To bring you home, home, home!"

"Home, little Fan?" returned the boy.

"Yes!" said the child, brimful of glee. "Home, for good and all. Home, for ever and ever. Father is so much kinder than he used to be, that home's like Heaven! He spoke so gently to me one dear night when I was going to bed, that I was not afraid to ask him once more if you might come home; and he said Yes, you should;

and sent me via motor to bring you back to Innsmouth! And you're to be a man!" said the child, opening her eyes, "and are never to come back here; but first, we're to be together all the Christmas long, and have the merriest time in all the world."

"You are quite a woman, little Fan!" exclaimed the boy.

She clapped her hands and laughed, and tried to touch his head; but being too little, laughed again, and stood on tiptoe to embrace him. Then she began to drag him, in her childish eagerness, towards the door; and he, nothing loth to go, accompanied her.

A terrible voice in the hall cried. "Bring down Master Scrooge's luggage, there!" and in the hall appeared the schoolmaster himself, who glared on Master Scrooge with a ferocious condescension, and threw him into a dreadful state of mind by shaking hands with him. He then conveyed him and his sister into his study, where the maps upon the wall, and the celestial and terrestrial globes in the windows, were waxy with cold. Old Scrooge found himself drawn to the maps just as he had been all those years ago. Hand drawn musings of Zobna and Lomar, even Hyperborea and Cimmeria.

Old Scrooge smiled, "My first glimpses of the forgotten realms. These drawings piqued my curiosity even as a child."

"They are inaccurate," grunted the Ghost, "but mortal maps often are."

Scrooge turned back to the office and watched the schoolmaster as he produced a decanter of curiously light wine, and a block of curiously heavy cake, and administered instalments of those dainties to the young people: at the same time, sending out a meagre servant to offer a glass of something to the postboy, who answered that he thanked the gentleman, but if it was the same tap as he had tasted before, he had rather not. Master Scrooge's luggage being by this time tied on to the top of the car (at the time a curiosity afforded only by his family), the children bade the schoolmaster good-bye right willingly; and getting into it, drove gaily down the garden-sweep: the quick wheels dashing the hoar-frost and snow from off the dark leaves of the evergreens like spray.

"Always a delicate creature, whom a breath might have withered," said the Ghost. "But she had a large heart."

"So she had," cried Scrooge. "You're right, Spirit. I cannot deny. The kindness she showed me in life I have mourned ever since her passing."

"She died a woman," said the Ghost, "and had, as I think, children."

"One child," Scrooge returned.

"True," said the Ghost. "Your nephew."

Scrooge seemed uneasy in his mind; and answered briefly, "Yes. Fred. He visited me at the University."

"Oh?" The Ghost seemed intrigued. If it knew of the events and merely quizzed to prompt discussion, it did not show.

"He invited me to Christmas dinner. I refused. I find his kindness…unsettling. Like a spectre of the past."

"He reminds you of your sister?"

"Very much so."

"And yet you remain distant?"

"I will not destroy his life as I did hers. I introduced her to Jacob, I brought her with us on our damned-fool escapades and I filled her mind with stories that I now find are unsettlingly true. What if he were to know that his mother survives, a ghastly hybrid of Gods living in an underwater city? What then? Now more than ever, I must keep my distance."

"You wish to protect him?" the Spirit asked.

"I must. He can never know of the horrors that took his family away from him." Scrooge was resolute.

Although they had but that moment left the school behind them, they were now in the busy thoroughfares of Innsmouth, where shadowy passengers passed and repassed; where cars and coaches battle for the way, and all the strife and tumult of a real city were. It was made plain enough, by the dressing of the shops, that here too it was Christmas time again; but it was evening, and the streets were lighted up.

The Ghost stopped at a certain warehouse door, and asked Scrooge if he knew it.

"Know it?" said Scrooge. "I worked here for a time. The happiest time. I required funding for my first piece of research. I took a job at Fezziwig's Warehouse with Jacob to help towards the costs!"

They went in. At sight of an old gentleman in sitting behind a high desk, that if he had been two inches taller he must have knocked his head against the ceiling, Scrooge cried in great excitement:

"Why, it's old Fezziwig! Bless his heart; it's Fezziwig alive again!"

Old Fezziwig laid down his pen, and looked up at the clock, which pointed to the hour of seven. He rubbed his hands; adjusted his capacious waistcoat; laughed all over himself, from his shows to his organ of benevolence; and called out in a comfortable, oily, rich, fat, jovial voice:

"Yo ho, there! Ebenezer! Jacob!"

Scrooge's former self, now grown a young man, came briskly in, accompanied by his fellow worker, a young Jacob Marley. How happy Scrooge was to see Jacob so full of life, in comparison to his ghastly encounter.

"No more work tonight. Christmas Eve, Jacob. Christmas, Ebenezer! Let's have the shutters up," cried old Fezziwig, with a sharp clap of his hands, "before a man can say, Jack Robinson!"

Old Scrooge laughed as he watched his younger self spring in to action. "You wouldn't believe how we went at it! We would charge into the street with the shutters -- one, two, three -- had 'em up in their places -- four, five, six -- barred 'em and pinned 'em -- seven, eight, nine -- and came back before you could have got to twelve, panting like race-horses. There was nothing we wouldn't have cleared away, or couldn't have cleared away, with old Fezziwig looking on. It was done in a minute. Every movable was packed off, as if it were dismissed from public life for evermore; the floor was swept and watered, fuel was heaped upon the fire; and the warehouse was as snug, and warm, and dry, and bright a ball-room, as you would desire to see upon a winter's night. Then, In would come a musician, in would come Mrs. Fezziwig, one vast substantial smile, and hundreds more for Fezziwig's Christmas Ball. In they all came, one after nother; some shyly, some boldly, some gracefully, some awkwardly, some pushing, some pulling; in they all came. Even Fan!"

Scrooge and the Spirit watched as the Ball broke in to full chorus before them. In the corner, Scrooge observed his sister, now a woman, sat with Young Jacob. "There!" Old Scrooge shouted, "This was the night they met. The night I introduced them. How happy they were for a while."

When the clock struck eleven, this domestic ball broke up. Mr and Mrs Fezziwig took their stations, one on either side of the door, and shaking hands with every person individually as he or she went out, wished him or her a Merry Christmas.

During the whole of this time, Scrooge had acted like a man out of his wits. His heart and soul were in the scene, and with his former self, sister and partner. He corroborated everything, remembered everything, enjoyed everything, and underwent the strangest agitation. It was not until now, when the bright faces of his former self and Jacob were turned from them, that he remembered the Ghost, and became conscious that it was looking full upon him, while the light upon its head burnt very clear.

"A small matter," said the Ghost, "to make this young couple so happy."

"Happy!" grunted Scrooge. "Did I make them so happy when our boat ruptured against Devil's Reef? Were they filled with delight when we capsized, Fan screaming, Jacob losing consciousness?"

"They are together now," the Spirit offered. Was this meant as reassurance?

"They are monsters," Scrooge retorted, cruelly, "They needn't have been had I not brought them out to satisfy my whim. Would that they could walk ashore as they once did, visit me without revealing their hideous vestiges, or reminisce fondly with their dear son who misses them greatly? I took all that from them."

"They were chosen and sacrificed. Their mixing saved those around them, even you, Scrooge. The festive cheer experienced by such pitiful creatures as those you watched here at this warehouse; they all feel Christmas joy because it is the wish of the Elder Gods that they be joyful." But the Spirit's explanation did not satiate Ebenezer Scrooge.

"Perhaps the Elder Gods are wrong," Scrooge spoke.

"Then you deny joy to the human race? Are they to suffer all year long? Should they make sense of their dream states, awaken the Gods who slumber in the far depths of this planet? Should they witness the dance of the Old Ones and understand it as a declaration of malice? What then, Scrooge? Should the Elder Gods the humans to their insanity? Are human minds capable of correlating what you have discovered?"

Scrooge was weary, the burden heavy on his consciousness. "Take me home, Spirit. Show me no more."

"One shadow more," the Ghost spoke and Fezziwig's warehouse began to quake and rumble.

"What is this? I wish to see no more. Why do you delight in torturing me?" But Scrooge's plea could not be heard over the rumbling. The warehouse brickwork shook and the wooden beams overhead began to split. "Spirit? What is this? I cannot recall…"

But before Scrooge could finish his sentence, the far wall was breached and sea water came rushing upon him. The room began to fill quickly and Scrooge shrieked in horror as he struggled to escape. He waded towards the door and tried the handle, but it was locked. He considered the breached wall as a means of escape, but the pressure of the filling water kept him from approaching. Within seconds, he had been swept from his feet and called out to the Spirit for help, but he was nowhere to be seen. Had he abandoned Ebenezer? Was this a slow death? He remembered the haunting words of Jacob Marley. *Cthulhu fhtagn.*

Cthulhu Rises.

Was this his end? A grisly, drowned end before being sacrificed to the Great One? He screamed in terror, but his screams were now cut short, as he was struggling to keep his head above water. The ceiling of the warehouse drew closer and closer and he now raised his arms in an attempt to prevent his head colliding with the beams. He struggled frantically to swim in a circle. Was the Spirit still here?

The ceiling was mere inches from his face now and the water levels continued to rise. He took his last gulps of air, filling his lungs in the hope of finding a means to escape underwater. One last gasp, and he ducked into the freezing cold, salty depths of the unnatural flood.

As his head disappeared under the water, his eyes were clouded. He struggled to adjust to seeing underwater and, to his surprise, found he was no longer in the warehouse. The murky depths revealed the interior of a small ship. The walls were no longer brick, but riveted, the tall glass windows now small portholes. Was this the last shadow of which the Spirit spoke? His final breath of air now caught in his throat as he realised his present location.

This was the ship that collided with Devil's Reef.

The night Fan had died.

He swam frantically for an open porthole and squeezed through, pulling himself free of the wreckage and thundering towards the surface as the vessel slowly sank beneath him. With a gasp, he burst to the surface of the water, searching the horizon for signs of life. He saw a body pop to the surface and bob in the crest of the waves and recognised it as his own.

"Ebenezer! Fan!" He heard the distant cries of Young Jacob, who he now spotted fighting the current, struggling towards the floating body of Young Ebenezer Scrooge. "Ebenezer!" The head of the Young Scrooge suddenly lifted from the wave as he heard his name called.

"Fan?" Young Scrooge asked, then shouted, "Fan! Where are you?"

"I'll find her!" Old Scrooge replied, with the abandon of a man who no longer accepts that he is a phantom. He fought the oncoming waves with reckless abandon as he searched the floating ruins of the sinking ship, desperately clawing to find his lost sister. In his peripheral vision, Young Scrooge and Marley now clung to each other, reassuring each other that they will find Fan and save her. But Old Scrooge, conscious of the vain attempts of both men to rescue their beloved Fan. Old Scrooge fought back tears for so long, but now they streamed down his old face, mingling with saltwater that carried him.

Down he dove, as deep as he could possibly fight, desperately hoping to reach the sinking wreck and drag his sister to safety at the surface. But the wreck was now gone, to fathoms deeper than a mortal man could swim without equipment. He could feel the pressure acting against his body and suddenly feared his own mortality. Could a shadow such as this kill him? He would surely find out, for he swam deeper down, regardless for his own wellbeing. He could see a faint shadow of the boat now, but knew he could never reach it. He stopped and watched the wreck sink out of sight, the last fading glimpse of hope to save his sister.

Scrooge later swore to me, that as he watched, he saw the speck of a wreckage suddenly surrounded by a number of man-like shapes. He saw them drag something from the wreck before it vanished from sight and as quickly as they had arrived, they were gone. Had the Spirit orchestrated such a sighting? Or had Scrooge genuinely witnessed his sister's salvation at the hands of the Deep Ones? Regardless of the authenticity of his experience, Scrooge undoubtedly saw the Deep Ones remove something from the wreck, whilst his younger self floundered on the surface, incapable and inconsolable.

"Remove me!" Scrooge wanted to shout, "Haunt me no longer!"

Yet he stayed and watch the black abyss below, swirling without need for breath in the endless ocean. And from those vast, black depths, a light began to grow forth. Scrooge watched fascinated as the warm glow grew, driving itself towards him from deep fathoms – perhaps from the many columned city of Y'ha-nthlei, perhaps from some vestige of another underwater populace – the light travelled at an uncanny rate and came bursting forth beneath him. At that moment, Scrooge realised that it was the Spirit, that he had heard his cry and was to remove him from this place. The light reached Scrooge and he held on to it, as much as he could, and found himself gripping the odd man-child which had presented itself as his guide.

The Spirit propelled Scrooge at unachievable speeds towards the surface of the water and Scrooge realised just how far down he had travelled. There was an explosion of sound as they burst through the surface of the water in to the sky, soaring over the wreckage and the Reef. Scrooge looked down and saw his young self and Jacob clambering on to the Reef, sobbing as they mourned the loss of Fan. He closed his eyes, not wanting to relive that feeling a moment longer.

"Why do you shield yourself from these events?" The Spirit asked.

"They cause me great pain. A pain that I have lived with ever since," Scrooge sobbed.

"But your sister survives."

"In a manner," Scrooge begrudgingly admitted.

"She is immortal."

"What good is her immortality when she is condemned to the water?" Scrooge asked.

"You are too quick to judge," the Spirit offered, "for what you consider condemnation was the sacrifice which humankind required that Christmas. She may have been lost to you, but her sacrifice helped satiate the Elder Gods. The Great Cthulhu rested peacefully that night."

"I will not be sacrificed," Scrooge shouted.

"So be it." The Spirit said, and then let go of Scrooge.

Ebenezer began to fall towards the Earth. He looked up and the Spirit had twinkled out, gone back to Betelgeuse to service his masters. Scrooge flayed pointlessly as he tumbled through the sky, the jagged rocks of Devil's Reef growing larger and larger beneath him. He covered his head, a desperate bid to prevent its splitting against those outcrops. He could hear the rush of the ground approaching and all of a sudden it was upon him.

He bounced on to his mattress, immediately opening his eyes in a state of surprise and elation. He was no longer on that dreaded reef. It was no longer 1917. He was home, and the clock had barely turned one.

Whether Scrooge fainted or fell in to a deep slumber, I cannot say. But Scrooge's head sunk in to his pillow and his sleep was undisturbed by dreams.

III

In my previous entry, I have explained – by means of the ghastly visit to Scrooge's past – how events leading up to this night have influenced Scrooge's attitude. At the start of my account, I told how I harboured some sympathy for Old Scrooge, for his story is a tragic one. To lose both his sister and dearest friend both at Christmas and both to Gods long considered gone from this planet was enough to drive any man to the brink of insanity. But not Scrooge, who shut himself off from the world and shunned seasonal festivities, for fear of being hurt once again.

What Scrooge tells of his next encounter is indeed strange, as it speaks less of Scrooge's actions – past or present – which you will see.

Awaking in the middle of a prodigiously tough snore, and sitting up in bed to get his thoughts together, Scrooge had no occasion to be told that the bell was again upon the stroke of the hour – this time at Two. He felt that he was restored to consciousness in the right nick of time, for the especial purpose of holding a conference with the second messenger despatched to him through Jacob Marley's intervention. But, finding that he turned uncomfortably cold when he began to wonder which of his curtains this new spectre would draw back, he put them every one aside with his own hands; and lying down again, established a sharp look-out all round the bed, for he wished to challenge the Spirit on the moment of its appearance, and did not wish to be taken by surprise, and made nervous.

Gentlemen of the free-and-easy sort, who plume themselves on being acquainted with a move or two, and being usually equal to the time-of-day, express the wide range of their capacity for adventure by observing that they are good for anything from pitch-and-toss to manslaughter; between which opposite extremes, no doubt, there lies a tolerably wide and comprehensive range of subjects. Without venturing for Scrooge quite as hardily as this, I don't mind calling on you to believe that he was ready for a good broad field of strange appearances, and that nothing between a baby and rhinoceros would have astonished him very much.

Now, being prepared for almost anything, he was not by any means prepared for nothing; and, consequently, when the Bell struck Two, and no shape appeared, he was taken with a violent fit of trembling. Five minutes, ten minutes, a quater of an hour went by, yet nothing came. All this time, he lay upon his bed, the very core and centre of a blaze of ruddy light, which streamed upon it when the clock proclaimed the hour; and which, being only light, was more alarming than a dozen ghosts, as he was powerless to make out what it meant, or would be at; and was sometimes apprehensive that he might be at that very moment an interesting case of spontaneous combustion, without having the consolation of knowing it. At last, however, he began to think that the source and secret of this ghostly light might be in the adjoining room - as you or I would have thought at first; for it is always the person not in the predicament who knows what ought to have been done in it, and would unquestionably have done it too. He looked to the doorway and, further tracing it, it seemed to shine. This idea taking full possession of his mind, he got up softly and shuffled in his slippers to the door.

The moment Scrooge's hand was on the lock, a strange voice called him by his name, and bade him enter. He obeyed.

It was his own room. There was no doubt about that. But it had undergone a surprising transformation. The walls and ceiling were so hung with living green, that it looked a perfect grove; from every part of which, bright gleaming berries glistened. The crisp leaves of holly, mistletoe, and ivy reflected back the light, as if so many little mirrors had been scattered there; and such a mighty blaze went roaring up the chimney, as that dull petrification of a hearth had never known in Scrooge's time, or Marley's, or for many and many a winter season gone. Heaped up on the floor, to form a kind of throne, were turkeys, geese, game, poultry, brawn, great joints of meat, sucking-pigs, long wreaths of sausages, mince-pies, plum-puddings, barrels of oysters, red-hot chesnuts, cherry-cheeked apples, juicy oranges, luscious pears, immense twelfth-cakes, and seething bowls of punch, that made the chamber dim with their delicious steam. In easy state upon this couch, there sat a jolly Giant, glorious to see: who bore a glowing torch, in shape not unlike Plenty's horn, and held it up, high up, to shed its light on Scrooge, as he came peeping round the door.

"Come in!" exclaimed the Ghost. "Come in. and know me better, man!"

Scrooge entered timidly, and hung his head before this Spirit. He was not the dogged Scrooge he had been; and though the Spirit's eyes were clear and kind, he did not like to meet them.

"How may I know you?" Scrooge asked, as he had the previous entity. Was this another Old One, removed from the charge of Azathoth?

"I have travelled far, from the dim green double star that glitters like a daemonic eye in the blackness beyond Abbith. I seek the servitude of my parentage, rejecting the cannibalistic ways of that distant star from which I travelled."

"Do you have a name?" Scrooge pressed. The Giant leaned in closer, his large furry beard began to writhe and Scrooge realised that each strand of hair was indeed a small tentacle, each one shifting and writhing independently on the Giant's face.

"I am the Ghost of Christmas Present," said the Spirit. "Look upon me!"

Scrooge reverently did so. It was clothed in one simple green robe, or mantle, bordered with white fur. This garment hung so loosely on the figure, that its capacious breast was bare, as if disdaining to be warded or concealed by any artifice. Its feet, observable beneath the ample folds of the garment, were also bare; and on its head it wore no other covering than a holly wreath, set here and there with shining icicles. Its dark brown curls were long and free: free as its genial face, its sparkling eye, its open hand, its cheery voice, its unconstrained demeanour, and its joyful air. Girded round its middle was an antique scabbard; but no sword was in it, and the ancient sheath was eaten up with rust.

"You have never seen the like of me before!" exclaimed the Spirit.

"Never," Scrooge made answer to it.

"You have never walked forth with my brothers, the star-spawn of Cthulhu, who spread the dreams of our sleeping father to those who wish it?" pursued the Phantom.

"I don't think I have," said Scrooge. "I am afraid I have not. Have you had many brothers, Spirit?"

"We have roamed your planet since our father, the Great Cthulhu Cthulhu first came. We are the reason why half the great temporary stars of history flared forth," said the Ghost.

It may occur to you that the flaring of a temporary star is very similar to the light described in Christianity, resulting in the discovery of the Son of God. It would appear, based upon the cryptic responses of this Elder God, that the basis for Christianity – and therefore Christmas itself – can be traced back to the Elder Gods themselves. But that debate is for another time, for scholars far more advanced than myself.

The Ghost of Christmas Present rose.

"Spirit," said Scrooge submissively, "conduct me where you will. I went forth earlier on compulsion, and I saw untold horrors which have shaped my life and now feel in a position to move past them. Tonight, if you have aught to teach me, let me profit by it."

"Touch my robe." The God commanded.

Scrooge did as he was told, and held it fast.

Holly, mistletoe, red berries, ivy, turkeys, geese, game, poultry, brawn, meat, pigs, sausages, oysters, pies, puddings, fruit, and punch, all vanished instantly. So did the room, the fire, the ruddy glow, the hour of night, and they stood in the city streets on Christmas morning, where (for the weather was severe) the people made a rough, but brisk and not unpleasant kind of music, in scraping the snow from the pavement in front of their dwellings, and from the tops of their houses: whence it was mad delight to the boys to see it come plumping down into the road below, and splitting into artificial little snow-storms.

The house fronts looked black enough, and the windows blacker, contrasting with the smooth white sheet of snow upon the roofs, and with the dirtier snow upon the ground; which last deposit had been ploughed up in deep furrows by the heavy wheels of cars and wagons; furrows that crossed and recrossed each other hundreds of times where the great streets branched off; and made intricate channels, hard to trace in the thick yellow mud and icy water. The sky was gloomy, and the shortest streets were choked up with a dingy mist, half thawed, half frozen, whose heavier particles descended in shower of sooty atoms, as if all the chimneys in Arkham had, by one consent, caught fire, and were blazing away to their dear hearts' content. There was nothing very cheerful in the climate or the town, and yet was there an air of cheerfulness abroad that the clearest summer air and brightest summer sun might have endeavoured to diffuse in vain.

For the people who were shovelling away on the housetops were jovial and full of glee; calling out to one another from the parapets, and now and then exchanging a facetious snowball -- better-natured missile far than many a wordy jest -- laughing heartily if it went right and not less heartily if it went wrong. A few shops remained open, selling their fresh wares to the freezing passers-by. There were great, round, pot-bellied baskets of chestnuts, shaped like the waistcoats of jolly old gentlemen, lolling at the doors, and tumbling out into the street in their apoplectic opulence. There were ruddy, brown-faced, broad-girthed Spanish Onions, shining in the fatness of their growth like Spanish Friars, and winking from their shelves in wanton slyness at the girls as they went by, and glanced demurely at the hung-up mistletoe. There were pears and apples, clustered high in blooming pyramids; there were bunches of grapes, made, in the shopkeepers' benevolence to dangle from conspicuous hooks, that people's mouths might water gratis as they passed. The very gold and silver fish, set forth among these choice fruits in a bowl, though members of a dull and stagnant-blooded race, appeared to know that there was something going on; and, to a fish, went gasping round and round their little world in slow and passionless excitement.

The Grocers, nearly closed, with perhaps two shutters down, or one; but through those gaps such glimpses! It was not alone that the scales descending on the counter made a merry sound, or that the twine and roller parted company so briskly, or that the canisters were rattled up and down like juggling tricks, or even that the blended scents of tea and coffee were so grateful to the nose, or even that the raisins were so plentiful and rare, the almonds so extremely white, the sticks of cinnamon so long and straight, the other spices so delicious, the candied fruits so caked and spotted with molten sugar as to make the coldest lookers-on feel faint and subsequently bilious. Nor was it that the figs were moist and pulpy, or that the French plums blushed in modest tartness from their highly-decorated boxes, or that everything was good to eat and in its Christmas dress; but the customers were all so hurried and so eager in the hopeful promise of the day, that they tumbled up against each other at the door, crashing their baskets wildly, and left their purchases upon the counter, and came running back to fetch them, and committed hundreds of the like mistakes, in the best humour possible; while the Grocer and his people were so frank and fresh that the polished hearts with which they fastened their aprons behind might have been their own, worn outside for general inspection. The sight of revellers appeared to interest the Spirit very much, for he stood with Scrooge beside him in a baker's doorway, and taking off the covers as their bearers passed, sprinkled incense on their dinners from his torch. It was a very uncommon kind of torch, for once or twice when there were angry words between some dinner-carriers who had jostled each other, he shed a few drops of water on them from it, and their good humour was restored directly. For they said, it was a shame to quarrel upon Christmas Day. And so it was!

"Is there a peculiar flavour in what you sprinkle from your torch?" asked Scrooge.

"There is. My own."

"Would it apply to any kind of dinner on this day?" asked Scrooge.

"To any kindly given. To a poor one most."

"I wonder, of all the beings in the many worlds about us that you may know of, why to a poor one most?" asked Scrooge.

"Because it needs it most."

"And what of the remainder of the year? Why Christmas?" Scrooge was curious, though he feared the answer.

"There are times during which we are at our most powerful, Christmas above all others. It is the time of year during which my father becomes restless and requires feeding to resume his slumber. We have greatest influence over mortal minds at such a time as this." The Giant's explanation brought many other unanswered questions to Scrooge's mind, but he asked just one.

"And the rest of the year?"

"Worship is enough to satiate our appetite until December whilst our father waits. *Ph'nglui mglw'nafh Cthulhu R'lyeh wgah'nagl fhtagn*."

The Giant had slipped mindlessly into the language of the Elder Ones. It was a phrase Scrooge had heard Marley repeat earlier that night, and a mantra often repeated by the Esoteric Order of Dagon – a cult that now ranks as the primary religion in Innsmouth. They were believed to sacrifice people to Dagon in return for limitless wealth. But Scrooge now understood that once a year, that limitless wealth was spread throughout this mortal realm.

"Forgive me if I am wrong, but there is an Order that kills in your name, or at least in that of your family," said Scrooge.

"There are some upon this earth of yours," returned the Spirit, "who lay claim to know us, and who do their deeds of passion, pride, ill-will, hatred, envy, bigotry, and selfishness in our name, who are as strange to us and all our kin, as if they had never lived. Remember that, and charge their doings on themselves, not us."

Scrooge promised that he would; and they went on, invisible, as they had been before, into the suburbs of the town. It was a remarkable quality of the Ghost (which Scrooge had observed at the baker's), that notwithstanding his gigantic size, he could accommodate himself to any place with ease; and that he stood beneath a low roof quite as gracefully and like a supernatural creature, as it was possible he could have done in any lofty hall.

Soon, the steeples called people to church and chapel, and few came, flocking through the streets in their best clothes. Significantly more so crowded towards a Masonic hall, and it was they who drew Scrooge's attention.

This was undoubtedly the Arkham home of The Esoteric Order of Dagon. Scrooge and Marley had been told of it by former Innsmouth residents, who described how it was undoubtedly a debased, quasi-pagan thing imported from the East a century before, at a time when the Innsmouth fisheries seemed to be going barren. Its persistence among a simple people was quite natural in view of the sudden and permanent return of abundantly fine fishing, and it soon came to be the greatest influence on the town, replacing Freemasonry altogether and taking up headquarters in the old Masonic Hall on New Church Green.

Scrooge had never noticed a chapter in Arkham before, and quizzed the Giant as to its legitimacy.

"These are the shadows of the present," The Giant offered, "Who is to blame if you have not witnessed that which is around you? You continue to pursue cities long forbidden to mortals, yet you are surprised by the formation of the Order in your town? You have brought them here, Scrooge, however inadvertently, you have led Arkham to worship our like."

With that, the Spirit led him straight to Scrooge's clerk's; for there he went, and took Scrooge with him, holding to his robe; and on the threshold of the door the Spirit smiled, and stopped to bless Bob Cratchit's dwelling with the sprinkling of his torch.

Then up rose Mrs Cratchit, Cratchit's wife and she laid the cloth, assisted by Belinda Cratchit, second of her daughters, while Master Peter Cratchit plunged a fork into the saucepan of potatoes. And now two smaller Cratchit's, boy and girl, came tearing in, screaming that outside the baker's they had smelt the turkey, and known it for their own; and basking in luxurious thoughts of sage-and-onion, these young Cratchit's danced about the table, and exalted Master Peter Cratchit to the skies, while he watched the stove as the potatoes bubbled up, knocking loudly on the saucepan-lid to be let out and peeled.

"What has ever got your precious father then." said Mrs Cratchit. "And your brother, Tiny Tim! And Martha wasn't as late last Christmas!"

"Here's Martha, mother!" said a girl, appearing as she spoke.

"Here's Martha, mother!" cried the two young Cratchits. "And she has the turkey!"

"How late you are, Martha," said Mrs Cratchit, kissing her a dozen times, and taking off her shawl and bonnet for her with officious zeal.

"We'd a deal of work to finish up last night," replied the girl, "and had to clear away this morning, mother!"

"Well! Never mind, you're home now," said Mrs Cratchit. "Sit down beside the fire, my dear, and have a warm."

"No, no! There's father coming," cried the two young Cratchits, who were everywhere at once. "Hide, Martha, hide!"

So Martha hid herself, and in came little Bob, the father, with at least three feet of comforter exclusive of the fringe, hanging down before him; and his threadbare clothes darned up and brushed, to look seasonable; and Tiny Tim upon his shoulder. Alas for Tiny Tim, he bore a little crutch, and had his limbs supported by an iron frame.

"Why, where's Martha?" cried Bob Cratchit, looking round.

"Not coming," said Mrs Cratchit.

"Not coming?" said Bob, with a sudden decline in his high spirits; for he had been Tim's blood horse all the way from church, and had come home rampant. "Not coming upon Christmas Day?"

Martha didn't like to see him disappointed, if it were only in joke; so she came out prematurely from behind the closet door, and ran into his arms, while the two young Cratchit's hustled Tiny Tim, and bore him off into the wash-house, that he might hear the pudding singing in the copper.

"And how did little Tim behave?" asked Mrs Cratchit, when she had rallied Bob on his credulity and Bob had hugged his daughter to his heart's content.

"As good as gold," said Bob, "and better. Somehow he gets thoughtful, sitting by himself so much, and thinks the strangest things you ever heard. He told me, coming home, that he hoped the people saw him in the church, because he was a cripple, and it might be pleasant to them to remember upon Christmas Day, who made lame beggars walk, and blind men see."

Bob's voice was tremulous when he told them this, and trembled more when he said that Tiny Tim was growing strong and hearty.

Old Scrooge was surprised, "I knew nothing of Bob's family."

"You asked him of them, surely?" The Giant said.

"Never."

"You forsake all company, Scrooge. Even that of your family. Again, you are too consumed with your work to even ask as to the wellbeing of your long time clerk's family. Well, you found the Gods you searched so long for. Will you still shun such company in the workplace?"

"I will ask of his family, and ask often."

"Would that you will ever get the chance again," The Giant teased. Scrooge refused to respond.

The sound of an active little crutch was heard upon the floor, and back came Tiny Tim before another word was spoken, escorted by his brother and sister to his chair beside the fire; and while Bob, turning up his cuffs, compounded some hot mixture in a jug with gin and lemons, and stirred it round and round and put it on the hob to simmer; Master Peter, and the two ubiquitous young Cratchit's went to fetch the turkey, with which they soon returned in high procession.

Such a bustle ensued that you might have thought a turkey the rarest of all birds; a feathered phenomenon, to which a black swan was a matter of course; and in truth it was something very like it in that house. Mrs Cratchit made the gravy (ready beforehand in a little saucepan) hissing hot; Master Peter mashed the potatoes with incredible vigour; Miss Belinda sweetened up the apple-sauce; Martha dusted the hot plates; Bob took Tiny Tim beside him in a tiny corner at the table; the two young Cratchit's set chairs for everybody, not forgetting themselves, and mounting guard upon their posts, crammed spoons into their mouths, lest they should shriek for turkey before their turn came to be helped. At last the dishes were set on, and grace was said. It was succeeded by a breathless pause, as Mrs Cratchit, looking slowly all along the carving-knife, prepared to plunge it in the breast; but when she did, and when the long expected gush of stuffing issued forth, one murmur of delight arose all-round the board, and even Tiny Tim, excited by the two young Cratchits, beat on the table with the handle of his knife, and feebly cheered.

There never was such a turkey. Bob said he didn't believe there ever was such a turkey cooked. Its tenderness and flavour, size and cheapness, were the themes of universal admiration. Eked out by apple-sauce and mashed potatoes, it was a sufficient dinner for the whole family; indeed, as Mrs Cratchit said with great delight (surveying one small atom of a bone upon the dish), they hadn't ate it all at last. Yet everyone had had enough, and the youngest Cratchit's in particular, were steeped in sage and onion seemingly to the eyebrows. But now, the plates being changed by Miss Belinda, Mrs Cratchit left the room alone to take the pudding up, and bring it in.

Scrooge observed the nervous excitement on Mrs Cratchit's face as she tended to the pudding. Suppose it should not be done enough, suppose it should break in turning out, suppose somebody should have got over the wall of the back-yard, and stolen it, while they were merry with the turkey: a supposition at which the two young Cratchit's became livid. All sorts of horrors were cheerily supposed. And all the while, Scrooge watched with delight as the family smiled and cheered together.

In half a minute Mrs Cratchit entered: flushed, but smiling proudly: with the pudding, like a speckled cannon-ball, so hard and firm, blazing in half of half-a-quartern of ignited brandy, and decorated with a Christmas holly stuck into the top.

"Oh, a wonderful pudding!" Bob Cratchit said, and calmly too, that he regarded it as the greatest success achieved by Mrs Cratchit since their marriage. Mrs Cratchit said that now the weight was off her mind, she would confess she had had her doubts about the quantity of flour.

At last the dinner was all done, the cloth was cleared, the hearth swept, and the fire made up. The compound in the jug being tasted, and considered perfect, apples and oranges were put upon the table, and a shovel-full of chestnuts on the fire. Then all the Cratchit family drew around the hearth while the chestnuts on the fire sputtered and cracked noisily. Then Bob proposed:

"A Merry Christmas to us all, my dears. God bless us!"

Which all the family re-echoed.

"God bless us every one!" said Tiny Tim, the last of all.

He sat very close to his father's side upon his little stool. Bob held his withered little hand in his, as if he loved the child, and wished to keep him by his side, and dreaded that he might be taken from him.

"Spirit," said Scrooge, with an interest he had never felt before, "tell me if Tiny Tim will live."

"I see a vacant seat," replied the Giant, "in the corner of the room. A crutch perfectly preserved. If these shadows remain, then the boy shall die."

"No, no," said Scrooge. "Oh, no, Spirit! Say he will be spared."

"If these shadows remain unaltered by the Future, none other of my race," returned the Giant, "will find him here. What then?"

"How can he be spared?" Scrooge begged, "Tell me how I may yet save him."

"This is not for me to tell," the Giant returned, "his fate is his own, just as yours will be your own. What choose you, Scrooge?"

Cthulhu fhtagn.

No, he would not become a sacrifice. He would remain here and help his clerk attend to Tiny Tim. Scrooge hung his head and was overcome with grief.

"Man," said the Giant, "if man you be in heart. Will you decide what men shall live and what men shall die? It may be that in the sight of R'lyeh, you are more worthless and less fit to live than millions like this poor man's child. Oh Great Cthulhu! To hear this insect pronounce life, whilst his hungry brothers amongst him turn to dust! Humankind is a pitiful race, sometimes."

Scrooge bent before the Giant's rebuke, and trembling cast his eyes upon the ground. But he raised them speedily, on hearing his own name.

"Mr Scrooge!" said Bob; "I'll give you Mr Scrooge, the Founder of the Feast!"

"The Founder of the Feast indeed!" cried Mrs Cratchit, reddening. "I wish I had him here. I'd give him a piece of my mind to feast upon, and I hope he'd have a good appetite for it."

"My dear," said Bob, "the children; Christmas Day."

"It should be Christmas Day, I am sure," said she, "on which one drinks the health of such an odious, stingy, hard, unfeeling man as Mr Scrooge. You know he is, Robert! Nobody knows it better than you do!"

"My dear," was Bob's mild answer, "Christmas Day."

"I'll drink his health for your sake and the Day's," said Mrs Cratchit, "not for his. Long life to him. A merry Christmas and a happy new year! He'll be very merry and very happy, I have no doubt!"

"But that he will not, my dear," Bob added.

"Oh? You'd stick up for him, Robert?" Mrs Cratchit retorted.

"Christmas time has been particularly hard for Mr Scrooge these past few years, what with his partner's death only recent. It's no surprise he shuns all company when he feels so accursed."

"Accursed?" Mrs Cratchit spat, "If he is so accursed, you should cease your employment with him now. I've heard people speak of the unnatural things that Ebenezer Scrooge studies, of his unholy opinions. I won't have them repeated in my house!" Mrs Cratchit paused, "Would that he had died rather than Mr Marley."

Scrooge quietly agreed. This wretched curse may have ended on that day and no more blood would be spilt. Perhaps the Gods would sleep more soundly without his continued presence and confounded interference.

"Mr Scrooge is on the verge of a scientific breakthrough," Bob offered his wife, "Should his funding be cleared, I've no doubt that Mr Scrooge will be able to prove…"

"Stop there, Robert." Mrs Cratchit was becoming irate, "I won't hear those names mentioned in this house."

"What, only down the street resides the Esoteric Order…"

"Enough! This town is taken with madness, Bob Cratchit, and you know it. It has become as warped and vile as Innsmouth, and that's a fact. I have heard some say that the founders of the Arkham chapel are Innsmouth folk, too. Strange and pale, they keep themselves indoors and are rarely seen during the day. Whatever happens within that hall is demonic."

"I have read Mr Scrooge's papers," Bob added, "I can vouch for their accuracy."

Tiny Tim nudged his father, "Is Dagon real, father?"

Mrs Cratchit leapt to her feet, "You see? Do you see what you have caused? You've filled poor Tim's mind with talk of outer space deities on celestial monstrosities. Do you wish this family committed?"

Scrooge was surprised, "I had no idea that Bob Cratchit subscribed to my theories. He's a smart boy."

"His son is smarter," the Giant spoke, "He is more suggestible. He reminds me of a young boy who once examined Hyperborean maps on his headmaster's wall."

"His mother doesn't approve?" asked Scrooge.

"Why would she? The only knowledge she has of the Elder Gods comes from a demented old fool who refuses to surface above his books. A man who has caused the death of at least two members of his immediate family and is now walking amongst them as a shade."

"Point taken," Scrooge nodded. Scrooge was clearly the Ogre of the family. The mention of his name cast a dark shadow on the party, which was not dispelled for full five minutes.

Bob Cratchit, kindly spoken as he was, turned the conversation back to Christmas cheer and soon his ill-timed toast of Ebenezer Scrooge was a distant memory. He toasted his wife, the lovely Mrs Cratchit, congratulating her on such a wonderful meal. The children drank the toast for her.

The night wore on, they were ten times merrier than before and Bob Cratchit told them how he had a situation in his eye for Master Peter, which would bring in, if obtained, a decent weekly wage for the young master. The two young Cratchit's laughed tremendously at the idea of Peter's being a man of business; and Peter himself looked thoughtfully at the fire from between his collars, as if he were deliberating what particular investments he should favour when he came into the receipt of such a bewildering income. Martha, who was a poor apprentice at a milliner's, then told them what kind of work she had to do, and how many hours she worked at a stretch, and how she meant to lie in bed tomorrow morning for a good long rest; tomorrow being a holiday she passed at home. Also how she had seen a countess and a lord some days before (whom had travelled to Massachusetts from England), and how the lord "was much about as tall as Peter;" at which Peter pulled up his collars so high that you couldn't have seen his head if you had been there. All this time the chestnuts and the jug went round and round; and bye and bye they had a song, about a lost child travelling in the snow, from Tiny Tim; who had a plaintive little voice, and sang it very well indeed.

They were happy, grateful, pleased with one another, and contented with the time; and when they faded, and looked happier yet in the bright sprinklings of the Giant's torch at parting, Scrooge had his eye upon them, and especially on Tiny Tim, until the last.

By this time it was getting dark, and snowing pretty heavily; and as Scrooge and the Giant went along the streets, the brightness of the roaring fires in kitchens, parlours, and all sorts of rooms, was wonderful. Here, the flickering of the blaze showed preparations for a cosy dinner, with hot plates baking through and through before the fire, and deep red curtains, ready to be drawn to shut out cold and darkness. There all the children of the house were running out into the snow to meet their married sisters, brothers, cousins, uncles, aunts, and be the first to greet them. Here, again, were shadows on the window-blind of guests assembling; and there a group of handsome girls, all hooded and fur-booted, and all chattering at once, tripped lightly off to some near neighbour's house; where, woe upon the single man who saw them enter -- artful witches, well they knew it -- in a glow!

But, if you had judged from the numbers of people on their way to friendly gatherings, you might have thought that no one was at home to give them welcome when they got there, instead of every house expecting company, and piling up its fires half-chimney high. Blessings on it, how the Giant exulted! How it bared its breadth of breast, and opened its capacious palm, and floated on, outpouring, with a generous hand, its bright and harmless mirth on everything within its reach. The very lamplighter, who ran on before, dotting the dusky street with specks of light, and who was dressed to spend the evening somewhere, laughed out loudly as the Giant passed: though little kenned the lamplighter that he had any company but Christmas.

And now, without a word of warning from the Giant, they stood upon a bleak and desert moor, where monstrous masses of rude stone were cast about, as though it were the burial-place of long forgotten beings; and water spread itself wheresoever it listed; or would have done so, but for the frost that held it prisoner; and nothing grew but moss and furze, and coarse, rank grass. Down in the west the setting sun had left a streak of fiery red, which glared upon the desolation for an instant, like a sullen eye, and frowning lower, lower, lower yet, was lost in the thick gloom of darkest night.

"What place is this?" asked Scrooge.

"A place where Miners live, who labour in the bowels of the earth," returned the Spirit. "But they know me. See!"

A light shone from the window of a hut, and swiftly they advanced towards it. Passing through the wall of mud and stone, they found a cheerful company assembled round a glowing fire. An old, old man and woman, with their children and their children's children, and another generation beyond that, all decked out gaily in their holiday attire. The old man, in a voice that seldom rose above the howling of the wind upon the barren waste, was singing them a Christmas song : it had been a very old song when he was a boy; and from time to time they all joined in the chorus. So surely as they raised their voices, the old man got quite blithe and loud; and so surely as they stopped, his vigour sank again.

The Spirit did not tarry here, but bade Scrooge hold his robe, and passing on above the moor, sped to the sea. To Scrooge's horror, looking back, he saw the last of the land, a frightful range of rocks, behind them; and his ears were deafened by the thundering of water, as it rolled, and roared, and raged among the dreadful caverns it had worn, and fiercely tried to undermine the earth.

Built upon a dismal reef of sunken rocks, some league or so from shore, on which the waters chafed and dashed, the wild year through, there stood a solitary lighthouse. Great heaps of sea-weed clung to its base, and storm-birds -- born of the wind one might suppose, as sea-weed of the water -- rose and fell about it, like the waves they skimmed.

But even here, two men who watched the light had made a fire, that through the loophole in the thick stone wall shed out a ray of brightness on the awful sea. Joining their horny hands over the rough table at which they sat, they wished each other Merry Christmas in their can of grog; and one of them: the elder, too, with his face all damaged and scarred with hard weather, as the figure-head of an old ship might be: struck up a sturdy song that was like a Gale in itself.

Again the Ghost sped on, above the black and heaving sea -- on, on -- until, being far away, as he told Scrooge, from any shore, they lighted on a ship. They stood beside the helmsman at the wheel, the look-out in the bow, the officers who had the watch; dark, ghostly figures in their several stations; but every man among them hummed a Christmas tune, or had a Christmas thought, or spoke below his breath to his companion of some bygone Christmas Day, with homeward hopes belonging to it. And every man on board, waking or sleeping, good or bad, had had a kinder word for another on that day than on any day in the year; and had shared to some extent in its festivities; and had remembered those he cared for at a distance, and had known that they delighted to remember him.

It was a great surprise to Scrooge, while listening to the moaning of the wind, and thinking what a solemn thing it was to move on through the lonely darkness over an unknown abyss, whose depths were secrets and as profound as Death. A deep that contained lost civilisations, not of this Earth, a deep in which slumbered Cthulhu himself, a horror beyond the reckoning of most mortal men. Scrooge later told how he could almost hear the quiet slumber of the great beast, the rhythmic breathing of an abomination set to destroy our world if penance was not paid upon Christmas Day. It was, therefore, a great surprise to Scrooge, while thus engaged, to hear a hearty laugh. It was a much greater surprise to Scrooge to recognise it as his own nephew's and to find himself in a bright, dry, gleaming room, with the Spirit standing smiling by his side, and looking at that same nephew with approving affability.

"Ha, ha!" laughed Scrooge's nephew. "Ha, ha, ha!"

If you should happen, by any unlikely chance, to know a man more blest in a laugh than Scrooge's nephew, all I can say is, I should like to have known him too. If I am ever in such a position again to meet such a gentleman, I would be happy to cultivate his acquaintance. Indeed, it is a fair, even-handed, noble adjustment of things, that while there is infection in disease and sorrow, there is nothing in the world so irresistibly contagious as laughter and good-humour. When Scrooge's nephew laughed in this way: holding his sides, rolling his head, and twisting his face into the most extravagant contortions: Scrooge's niece, by marriage, laughed as heartily as he. And their assembled friends being not a bit behindhand, roared out lustily.

"Ha, ha! Ha, ha, ha, ha!"

"He said that Christmas was a humbug, as I live!" cried Scrooge's nephew. "He believed it too!"

"More shame for him, Fred!" said Scrooge's niece, indignantly.

"He's a comical old fellow," said Scrooge's nephew, "that's the truth: and not so pleasant as he might be. However, his offences carry their own punishment, and I have nothing to say against him."

"I have no patience with him," observed Scrooge's niece. Scrooge's niece's sisters, and all the other ladies, expressed the same opinion.

"Oh, I have!" said Scrooge's nephew. "I am sorry for him; I couldn't be angry with him if I tried. Often I saw Old Uncle Ebenezer before my father's passing, and he was always so sad. It was always that he blamed himself for mother's death and the loss of father pushed him to the very brink of despair. And so he hides himself from the world, missing the most fondest of days and the most cherished of recent memories; Christmastime. And though we laugh to hear him call it such a thing as a 'Humbug', others would have you believe him to be the Devil himself, but this satiates the old fellow. And if his whims are considered ill, who suffers by them? Himself, always. Here, he takes it into his head to dislike us, and he won't come and dine with us. What's the consequence? He doesn't lose much of a dinner!"

The revellers all laugh to hear it be called so.

"Indeed, I think he loses a very good dinner," interrupted Scrooge's niece. Everybody else said the same, and they must be allowed to have been competent judges, because they had just had dinner; and, with the dessert upon the table, were clustered round the fire, by lamplight.

"Well! I'm very glad to hear it," said Scrooge's nephew, "because I haven't great faith in these young housekeepers."

"Do go on, Fred," said Scrooge's niece, clapping her hands. "He never finishes what he begins to say. He is such a ridiculous fellow!"

Scrooge's nephew revelled in another laugh, and as it was impossible to keep the infection off, his example was unanimously followed.

"I was only going to say," said Scrooge's nephew, "that the consequence of his taking a dislike to us, and not making merry with us, is, as I think, that he loses some pleasant moments, which could do him no harm. I am sure he loses pleasanter companions than he can find in his own thoughts, either in his mouldy old office, or his dusty chambers. I mean to give him the same chance every year, whether he likes it or not, for I pity him. He may rail at Christmas till he dies, but he can't help thinking better of it -- I defy him -- if he finds me going there, in good temper, year after year, and saying Uncle Scrooge, how are you?"

"Hear, hear!" came a voice from the assembled guests and they raised a glass.

"To Uncle Scrooge. Merry Christmas!"

"Uncle Scrooge!"

Old Ebenezer hung his head as he watched the revellers drink their toast. "It is too late now to take back the unkind words that I spoke to Fred. But I shall make amends. He is my only family and O, how he reminds me of my dear sister and Jacob."

"Moreso than you may think," The Giant grinned, "For we linger not to lament your unkindness. Master Frederick has too much of his father in him."

After tea, they had some music. Scrooge's niece played well upon the harp; and played among other tunes a simple little air which had been familiar to the child who fetched Scrooge from the boarding-school, as he had been reminded by the Ghost of Christmas Past. When this strain of music sounded, all the things that Ghost had shown him, came upon his mind; he softened more and more; and thought that if he could have listened to it often, years ago, he might have cultivated the kindnesses of life for his own happiness with his own hands, without resorting to the sexton's spade that buried Jacob Marley.

But they didn't devote the whole evening to music. After a while, they began to play games and Scrooge watched on in delight. It was not until the third game that Scrooge noticed the absence of his dear nephew Fred, who had absconded to his study, whereupon Ebenezer found him.

"This is what you speak of, Spirit?" asked Scrooge.

"A curious boy," mused the Giant, "A fellow scholar, no doubt."

Fred stood poised atop a large map of the South Pacific. His finger traced shipping paths as he noted down a series of calculations. Scrooge watched the twinkle in his young nephew's eyes as he darted from point to point and scribbled furiously in a notebook.

How should Scrooge feel to see his nephew so engaged? Proud? No. Scrooge's expression was one of fear. So many already taken, all sacrificed to the cruel gods who dwell above, below and in dimensions hitherto unknown to man. Now his nephew, an innocent, born of the love of the two people whom Scrooge held most dear, yet another willing participant in the discovery of such horrors as those that have guided Scrooge this night.

The door to the study opened and Scrooge's niece entered, looking sullen. "You have left the party," she stated. Fred did not impart a glance toward her.

"A few minutes more, my love, and I shall return," he told her. "I have need to collect my musings before they vanish."

She approached the map, but Fred quickly withdrew it from his desk, stuffing it in to the nearest drawer. As he looked upon her, guiltily, she cried, "R'lyeh? Again? Fred, how much longer must we indulge in these flights of fancy?"

"I will not discuss this," he ordered, "Return to the party. I shall be along presently."

"Are we to become like him? Taunted and isolated by all, save the Order? And if you have located the ruins, what then? Are we to lose the house for yet another tome of prophecies and half-truths?"

Scrooge looked to the bookcase, a fascinating array of books and tomes sat awkwardly on the shelf. Some had belonged to Jacob, for certain. An unfamiliar, yet incidentally inaccurate, *Necronomicon* lay atop a pile of books recently rifled.

"I am certain that if I take my findings to Uncle Scrooge at Miskatonic, we can apply for funding and take an expedition to…"

"No, Fred." Scrooge's niece silenced him, "This research was, in part, responsible for the loss of both your parents. I will not allow you to be consumed like your Uncle Scrooge. Return to the party, at once, and let us leave this whole dreadful research to him."

"I can help him."

"And you will be lost, like all others whom he has loved. I fear the path you tread may lead you to him sooner than you think."

Fred looked puzzled, "How so?"

"You have lost me, Fred. In a more humane way, perhaps, but still I am lost." Scrooge watched helplessly as his niece solemnly walked from the room. "Farewell, Frederick. May you be happy with the life you have chosen."

"No!" Scrooge shouted, "Go after her, boy! Do not make the mistakes I have made! The horrors which you hope to discover only lead to despair and misery. Go to her and pay no more heed to my work! Spirit! Spirit, how may I alter what transpires here?"

The Giant gave no comfort. He turned from the scene and Scrooge followed, pleading, but the scene had now passed off in the breath of Scrooge's last spoken word and he and the Giant were again upon their travels.

"Will you not speak to me?" Scrooge cried, "Will you not impart any wisdom? Why show me these shadows if I am not to overcome them?"

"Cthulhu fhtagn," the Giant offered as his only response.

Cthulhu rises.

The night wore on.

Much they saw, and far they went, and many homes they visited, but always with a happy end. The Spirit stood beside sick beds, and they were cheerful; on foreign lands, and they were close at home; by struggling men, and they were patient in their greater hope; by poverty, and it was rich. In alms-house, hospital, and jail, in misery's every refuge, where vain man in his little brief authority had not made fast the door and barred the Spirit out, he left his blessing, and taught Scrooge his precepts.

It was a long night, if it were only a night; but Scrooge had his doubts of this, because the Christmas Holidays appeared to be condensed into the space of time they passed together. It was strange, too, that while Scrooge remained unaltered in his outward form, the Ghost grew older, clearly older. Scrooge had observed this change, but never spoke of it, until they stood together in an open place, he noticed that its hair was grey.

"Are Spirits' lives so short?" asked Scrooge.

"My life in this form, in this dimension, is very brief," replied the Ghost. "It ends tonight."

"Tonight!" cried Scrooge.

"Tonight at midnight."

"And then?" Scrooge asked.

The Giant did not answer, but Scrooge knew.

Cthulhu fhtagn…

"This fleeting life, in which you gaze upon the merriment of mankind, why do you do this?" Scrooge asked of the Giant, who stopped.

"I honour my father, The Great Old One. I spread his waking dreams. In return, we now prepare for our recompense."

Scrooge shuddered, "And who will that be?"

"The time is drawing near," the Giant offered as reply.

The chimes were ringing the three quarters past eleven at that moment and Scrooge watched as the dusty, dying flesh of the Giant crumbled from his face. It was an horrific sight, to be sure, to see a man age and wither to dust before one's eyes. Scrooge struggled to stifle a scream and avoid swooning as the bones of the Giants crept in to view as his eyes sank and lips rotted away to bare teeth. He averted his gaze from this chilling display and noticed something within the Giant's robe that drew his attention.

"Forgive me if I am not justified in what I ask," said Scrooge, looking intently at the Spirit's robe, "but I see something strange, and not belonging to yourself, protruding from your robe. Is it a foot or a claw?"

"It might be a claw, for the flesh there is upon it," was the Giant's reply. "Look here."

From the folding's of its robe, it brought two children; wretched, abject, frightful, hideous, miserable. They knelt down at its feet, and clung upon the outside of its garment with what appeared to be arms. Yet, Scrooge noticed an unnatural movement in their limbs, as if disjointed. He gazed closer.

Their limbs were thick, flesh coloured tentacles. They curled wretchedly around the Giant like the tentacles of a squid and Scrooge recoiled in panic.

"Look upon them!" exclaimed the Ghost, but Scrooge turned away. "Down here! Gaze upon them, Scrooge!"

They were a boy and girl, or they may have been were it not for their grotesque limbs. Yellow, meagre, ragged, scowling; but prostrate, too, in their humility. Where graceful youth should have filled their features out, and touched them with its freshest tints, a stale and shrivelled hand, like that of age, had pinched, and twisted them, and pulled them into shreds. Where angels might have sat enthroned, devils lurked, and glared out menacing. No change, no degradation, no perversion of humanity, in any grade, through all the mysteries of wonderful creation, has monsters half so horrible and dreadful.

Scrooge started back, appalled. Having them shown to him in this way, he tried to say they were fine children, but the words choked themselves, rather than be parties to a lie of such enormous magnitude.

"Are they yours, Spirit?" Scrooge could say no more.

"They are mine," spoke a voice that was familiar, but did not belong to the Giant. Scrooge turned and Jacob Marley stepped forth from the fog.

"Jacob?" Scrooge replied through his nausea, "Is this true?"

"Their purpose has yet to be fulfilled," Jacob said.

"And that would be?"

"They are Man. I should say, they shall be Man," said Jacob Marley, looking down upon them. "See how they cling to their creator? The giver of life?" Indeed, the creatures still held to the rapidly decaying standing corpse of the Giant. "Just as Man has ever done, yet this time they cling to a tangible god. A tangible entity, capable of creating life, of manipulating life to create a mankind capable of greatness yet fastidious in their servitude to the Old Ones who grant us this gift."

"Abominations!" This was all Scrooge could muster.

"How so? They cling to their gods and appeal from their fathers for knowledge, for their names are thus; This boy is Ignorance. This girl is Want."

Scrooge averted his eyes from them. "They are monstrous."

"They are what you sought. They are what you have encouraged of all that you have taught and mentored. You entreat the Old Ones and this is the consequence. Ignorance and Want; Beware them both, and all of their degree, but most of all beware this boy, for on his brow I see that written which is Doom, unless the writing be erased. Deny it!" cried Jacob, stretching out his hand towards the city. "Slander those who tell it ye!"

"What must I do, Jacob?" cried Scrooge.

The bell struck twelve.

Scrooge was startled by the final collapse to ashes of the Giant. A gentle breeze drew his remnants across the city. When Scrooge turned back to Marley, he was rounding a corner.

Scrooge flew in pursuit, desperate not to be left to the horrors of his final visitor. He turned the corner and saw Jacob Marley vanish in to the distant fog. He further pursued Marley, though the fog was so thick that once within Scrooge could not see. Let it be recorded here that no such fog was recorded on Christmas Eve in Massachusetts. Wheresoever this ghastly fog arose from, we can only assume to be the same place as Scrooge's otherworldly deities.

Scrooge looked about him for the ghost of Jacob Marley, and saw it not. As the last stroke ceased to vibrate, the fog began to lift and a great sea breeze blew across him. Scrooge shivered, less from the chill but from the chilling sight which arose before him from the waters.

This was no longer Arkham. Scrooge stood before Innsmouth Harbour and the sea mist began to take the form of a solemn Phantom, draped and hooded, coming, like a mist along the ground, towards him.

IV

The Phantom slowly, gravely, silently approached. It was carried upon the waves and as the figure was calmly washed upon the shore, it glided effortlessly up on to the stone with ghoulish grace. When it came, Scrooge bent down upon his knee; for in the very air through which this Spirit moved it seemed to scatter gloom and mystery. Onward it approached and Scrooge stayed bowed in fealty. Was he frozen there by some magic? He dared not try to rise, for fear that his legs may buckle under the horror of such a meagre attempt of escape. Instead, he watched as this, the most mysterious yet most menacing of the Phantoms approached.

It was shrouded in a deep black garment, which concealed its head, its face, its form, and left nothing of it visible save one outstretched hand, which was claw-like, wizened and stiff as though some rigor mortis had already possessed it. The limb was blackened, by bruising or rot or a combination thereof. Against the dark of the night and the black of the Phantom's shroud, Scrooge could barely make out the full shape of this protuberance, yet he knew it was pointed towards him, reaching for him like the antennae of some vast space insect.

It was within reach now, so close to his face. He closed his eyes, not wishing to see a moment more.

He felt that it was tall and stately now that it stood beside him, and that its mysterious presence filled him with a solemn dread. He knew no more, for the Spirit neither spoke nor moved. He listened to the creak of the outstretched arm as it was withdrawn. It sounded like stretching leather.

"I am in the presence of the Ghost whose coming was foretold? The final Ghost?" said Scrooge.

The Spirit answered not, but pointed onward with its pointed, gnarled hand.

"You are about to show me shadows of the things that have not happened, but will happen in the time before us," Scrooge pursued. "Is that so, Spirit?"

The upper portion of the garment was contracted for an instant in its folds, as if the Spirit had inclined its head. That was the only answer he received.

Although well used to ghostly company by this time, Scrooge feared the silent shape so much that his legs trembled beneath him, and he found that he could hardly stand when he prepared to follow it. The Spirit paused a moment, as observing his condition, and giving him time to recover.

But Scrooge was all the worse for this. It thrilled him with a vague uncertain horror, to know that behind the dusky shroud, there were ghostly eyes intently fixed upon him, while he, though he stretched his own to the utmost, could see nothing but a spectral hand and one great heap of black.

"Ghost of the Future!" he exclaimed, "I fear you more than any spectre I have seen. But as I know your purpose is to do me good, and as I hope to live to be another man from what I was, I am prepared to bear you company, and do it with a thankful heart. Will you not speak to me?"

It gave him no reply. The hand was pointed straight before them.

Scrooge was unsettled. The predecessors to this Phantom had spoken, albeit cryptically, of themselves. Whilst it had provided little in the way of comfort, their discourse had gone some way towards easing his trepidation over what he was to see.

"Lead on!" said Scrooge. "Lead on! The night is waning fast, and it is precious time to me, I know. Lead on, Spirit!"

The Phantom moved away as it had come towards him. Scrooge followed in the shadow of its dress, which bore him up, he thought, and carried him along.

They scarcely seemed to enter the city of Innsmouth; for the city rather seemed to spring up about them, and encompass them of its own act. But there they were, in the heart of it; on Water Street, amongst the merchants; who hurried up and down, and counted the money in their pockets, and conversed in groups, and looked at their watches, and so forth, as Scrooge had seen them often at the Arkham markets.

The Spirit stopped beside one little knot of business men. Observing that the hand was pointed to them, Scrooge advanced to listen to their talk. They stood beneath a board which read 'James Leader, Fish Merchants'.

"No," said the proprietor, Mr Leader, to his companion, "I don't know much about it, either way. I only know he's dead."

"That's as no surprise," said the other. "When was this?"

"Last week, I believe."

"Why, what was the matter with him?" asked the customer, taking a vast quantity of snuff out of a very large snuff-box. "To swim out in to the harbour like that?"

"God knows," said Mr Leader, with a yawn, "Not that he was the first, mind. There have been a few such tragedies. Always around such a time as Christmas, too."

"Such a shame," the customer offered, "His poor family."

"Family?" scoffed Mr Leader, "That's what makes this whole event so queer, for he had only one family member still living. An estranged one, at that. Lived in Arkham, someplace towards the University, as far as I can gather."

"Lived?" asked the astute customer.

"Aye, he did, until hearing of the passing of the last of his bloodline. Upon notification, he went raving mad and was confined to the asylum in Arkham. Kept raving about fish gods and other ungodly creatures, from what I hear. One morning, the orderly approaches his room and he's gone, the bars on his windows torn asunder and no trace of the gentleman in question."

"He forced the bars? What strength!" The customer was enraptured with Mr Leader's story.

"A friend of mine, an employee of the Arkham Police Department, tells me that the bars appeared to have been torn from the outside, as if a great jailbreak had taken place! But I don't attribute that story to anything other than idle gossip. I prefer facts, which are thus; the old gentleman was found floating face down in the harbour late last night. Drowned, sir. Be it as a miscalculated bid to search for his dead nephew or suicide, I could not possibly speculate."

"Who is this of which these gentlemen speak?" Scrooge asked of the Phantom, but received no reply.

"Was he wealthy?" asked the customer, unaware of the shadow of Scrooge stood before him.

"Not by most accounts," replied Mr Leader, "but well enough endowed to spend his time solely on research."

"What has he done with his money, then, if there are no surviving family members?" asked the red-faced customer with a pendulous excrescence on the end of his nose that shook like the gills of a turkey-cock.

"I haven't heard," said Mr Leader, yawning again. "Left it to his Department, perhaps. He hasn't left it to me. That's all I know."

This pleasantry was received with a general laugh.

"It's likely to be a very cheap funeral," said the same speaker; "for upon my life I don't know of anybody to go to it. Suppose we make up a party and volunteer?"

"Travel to Arkham?"

"He's to be buried alongside his family, here in Innsmouth," Mr Leader observed.

"I don't mind going if a lunch is provided," observed the gentleman with the excrescence on his nose. "But I must be fed, if I make one."

Another laugh.

"Well, I am the most disinterested among you, after all," said Mr Leader, "for I never wear black gloves, and I never eat lunch. But I'll offer to go, if anybody else will."

Not another word. That was their meeting, their conversation, and their parting.

Scrooge was at first inclined to be surprised that the Spirit should attach importance to conversations apparently so trivial; but feeling assured that they must have some hidden purpose, he set himself to consider what it was likely to be. They could scarcely be supposed to have any bearing on the death of Jacob, his old partner, for that was Past, and this Ghost's province was the Future. Nor could he think of any one immediately connected with himself, to whom he could apply them. But nothing doubting that to whomsoever they applied they had some latent moral for his own improvement, he resolved to treasure up every word he heard, and everything he saw; and especially to observe the shadow of himself when it appeared. For he had an expectation that the conduct of his future self would give him the clue he missed, and would render the solution of these riddles easy.

Onward to Arkham, the Phantom took him, and to his own offices at Miskatonic University. He looked about in that very place for his own image; but another man stood in his accustomed corner, and though the clock pointed to his usual time of day for being there, he saw no likeness of himself among the multitudes that poured in through the doors. It gave him little surprise, however; for he had been revolving in his mind a change of life, and thought and hoped he saw his new-born resolutions carried out in this.

Quiet and dark, beside him stood the Phantom, with its outstretched, dead hand. When he roused himself from his thoughtful quest, he fancied from the turn of the hand, and its situation in reference to himself, that the Unseen Eyes were looking at him keenly. It made him shudder, and feel very cold.

They left the busy scene, and went into an obscure part of the University, where Scrooge had never penetrated before, although he recognised its situation. The staff quarters, home to Miskatonic's cleaners and caretakers. Not often were the academic staff required to come to this particularly dark part of the University. Here, in the bowels of the University, were secrets bred and hidden in mountains of unseemly rags. Sitting in among the wares he dealt in, was a grey-haired rascal, nearly seventy years of age; who had screened himself from the cold air without and smoked his pipe in all the luxury of calm retirement.

Scrooge and the Phantom came into the presence of this man, just as a woman with a heavy bundle slunk into the room. But she had scarcely entered, when another woman, similarly laden, came in too; and she was closely followed by a man in faded black, who was no less startled by the sight of them, than they had been upon the recognition of each other. After a short period of blank astonishment, in which the old man with the pipe had joined them, they all three burst into a laugh.

"Let the charwoman alone to be the first!" cried she who had entered first. "Let the laundress alone to be the second; and let the undertaker's man alone to be the third. Look here, old Joe, here's a chance! If we haven't all three met here without meaning it!"

"You couldn't have met in a better place," said old Joe, removing his pipe from his mouth. "Come into the parlour. You were made free of it long ago, you know; and the other two aren't strangers. Stop till I shut the door of the shop. Ah! There isn't such a rusty bit of metal in the place as its own hinges, I believe; and I'm sure there's no such old bones here, as mine. Ha, ha! We're all suitable to our calling, we're well matched. Come into the parlour. Come into the parlour."

While he did this, the woman who had already spoken threw her bundle on the floor, and sat down in a flaunting manner on a stool; crossing her elbows on her knees, and looking with a bold defiance at the other two.

"What odds then! What odds, Mrs Dilber?" said the woman. "Every person has a right to take care of themselves. He always did!"

"That's true, indeed!" said the laundress. "No man more so."

"Why then, don't stand staring as if you were afraid, woman; who's the wiser? We're not going to pick holes in each other's coats, I suppose?"

"No, indeed!" said Mrs Dilber and the man together. "We should hope not."

"Very well, then!" cried the woman. "That's enough. Who's the worse for the loss of a few things like these? Not a dead man, I suppose."

"No, indeed!" said Mrs Dilber, laughing.

"If he wanted to keep 'em after he was dead, a wicked old screw," pursued the woman, "why wasn't he natural in his lifetime? If he had been, he'd have had somebody to look after him when he was committed to the nut house. Maybe then, he would never have struck out to the port and caught his death!"

"It's the truest word that ever were spoke," said Mrs Dilber. "It's a judgment on him."

"I wish it was a little heavier judgment," replied the woman; "and it should have been, you may depend upon it, if I could have laid my hands on anything else. A strange old master he was, never spoke, never smiled. Cursed, he was. Open that bundle, old Joe, and let me know the value of it. Speak out plain. I'm not afraid to be the first, nor afraid for them to see it. We know pretty well that we were helping ourselves, before we met here, I believe. It's no sin. Open the bundle, Joe."

But the gallantry of her friends would not allow of this; and the man in faded black, mounting the breach first, produced his plunder. It was not extensive. A seal or two, a pencil-case, a pair of sleeve-buttons, and a brooch of no great value, were all. They were severally examined and appraised by old Joe, who chalked the sums he was disposed to give for each, upon the wall, and added them up into a total when he found there was nothing more to come.

"That's your account," said Joe, "and I wouldn't give another dime, if I were to be boiled for not doing it. Who's next?"

Mrs Dilber was next. Sheets and towels, a little wearing apparel and a few boots. Her account was stated on the wall in the same manner.

"I always give too much to ladies. It's a weakness of mine, and that's the way I ruin myself," said old Joe. "That's your account. If you asked me for another penny, and made it an open question, I'd repent of being so liberal and knock off a nickel."

"And now undo my bundle, Joe," said the first woman.

Joe went down on his knees for the greater convenience of opening it, and having unfastened a great many knots, dragged out a large and heavy tome.

"What do you call this?" said Joe. "Books!"

"Ah!" returned the woman, laughing and leaning forward on her crossed arms. "Books! Fine tomes they are. Rare and valuable!"

"You expect me to find means to sell these back to the campus?" asked Joe.

"Yes I do," replied the woman. "Why not?"

"You were born to make your fortune," said Joe, "and you'll certainly do it. But how am I to sell University property without drawing undue attention?"

"I certainly shan't hold my hand, when I can get anything in it by reaching it out, for the sake of such a man as He was, I promise you, Joe," returned the woman coolly. "the housekeepers at Harvard would show particular interest in such valuable a collection."

"I shall make enquiries of my opposite," Joe pondered, "let us hope the Miskatonic doesn't notice their absence beforehand."

"Don't you be afraid of that," returned the woman. "I an't so fond of his company that I'd loiter about him for such things, if there were a chance of being caught!"

Scrooge listened to this dialogue in horror. As they sat grouped about their spoil, in the scanty light afforded by the old man's lamp, he viewed them with a detestation and disgust, which could hardly have been greater, though they had been obscene demons, marketing the corpse itself.

"Ha, ha!" laughed the same woman, when old Joe, producing a flannel bag with money in it, told out their several gains upon the ground. "This is the end of it, you see! He frightened every one away from him when he was alive, to profit us when he was dead!"

"Spirit!" said Scrooge, shuddering from head to foot. "I see, I see. The case of this unhappy man might be my own. My life tends that way, now. Merciful Heaven, what is this!"

He recoiled in terror, for the scene had changed, and now he almost touched a table: a cold, metallic table on which, beneath a ragged sheet, there lay something covered up, which, though it was dumb, announced itself in awful language.

The room was very dark, too dark to be observed with any accuracy, though Scrooge glanced round it in obedience to a secret impulse, anxious to know what kind of room it was. It was tiled and clinical, cold and silent. A pale light, rising in the outer air, fell straight upon the bed; and on it, plundered and bereft, unwatched, unwept, uncared for, was the body of this man.

Scrooge glanced towards the Phantom. Its steady hand was pointed to the head. The cover was so carelessly adjusted that the slightest raising of it, the motion of a finger upon Scrooge's part, would have disclosed the face. He thought of it, felt how easy it would be to do, and longed to do it; but had no more power to withdraw the veil than to dismiss the spectre at his side.

"Am I to examine this poor soul?" Scrooge asked, "Is this the wretched creature washed upon the shores of Innsmouth? Your predecessors showed me the danger of my curious research. They showed me the horrors which will arise in pursuit of such objectives as R'lyeh and Y'ha-nthlei. Was this man similarly obsessed with the stories which have led me to your terrifying company? Is this yet another example of how the meddling of man may bring rise to the Great Old One?"

Cthulhu fhtagn…

"Speak to me, Spirit! Would that this man could speak now, what wisdom would he impart to me? What would be his foremost thoughts? Would he speak of the Esoteric Order of Dagon, perhaps? His studies in to such lore have led him to a rich end, truly. Not a man, a woman, or a child, to say that he was kind to them in this or that, and for the memory of one kind word I will be kind to him."

The Phantom stretched out is hand and pointed to the covered head of the corpse on the slab.

"I understand you," Scrooge returned, "and I would do it, if I could. But I have not the power, Spirit. I have not the power."

Again it seemed to look upon him.

"Spirit!" he said, "this is a fearful place. In leaving it, I shall not leave its lesson, trust me. Let us go!"

The Phantom turned from Scrooge and floated in to the shadows, beckoning with its leathery, claw-like appendage. Scrooge approached the Phantom, who spread its dark robe before him for a moment, like a wing; and withdrawing it, revealed a clifftop by dusk.

Seagulls cawed and fled towards the sea, the waves crashed against the cliffs below. Scrooge looked out upon the waves and recognised Innsmouth Harbour. A far speck on the horizon marked Devil's Reef. Behind him, the deep shadows of the city itself.

And the sound of approaching footsteps.

They were hurried. Scrooge's eyes darted from shadowy street to street as he sought the source of the approach. Suddenly, a young man darted out from an alleyway in to the open and started a dash toward the cliff upon which stood Scrooge. The boy was in his twenties, his features hidden in darkness. His erratic breathing confirmed that his pursuit, for Scrooge presumed from the backwards glances as he ran that he was being pursued, had been long and frantic.

He ran to the edge of the clifftop and Scrooge had to stifle a cry, still unused to his part in such proceedings. Could he prevent this young gentleman from falling to his death?

The young man stood looking down at the rocks below as the sound of scuffling now emanated from the shadows from which he had dashed. He turned and watched as shadows began to form in the alleyways of the nearest streets and Scrooge watched also, in terror.

I scarcely need to tell you that at this point, Scrooge was prepared for the worst, and really ought to have been prepared considering what had seen before, be that the demonic Jacob Marley or the variety of unholy creatures that had visited him during his night. Scrooge could not make out any particular shape as he watched the approaching shadows until the raucous clamour came loudly from a point obviously straight ahead.

As the pursuing creatures stepped in to the moonlight, still in restless pursuit of the young boy now pressed against the edges of the clifftop, Scrooge saw them in a limitless stream - flopping, hopping, croaking, bleating - surging inhumanly through the spectral moonlight in a grotesque, malignant saraband of fantastic nightmare. And some of them had tall tiaras of nameless whitish-gold metal . . . and some were strangely robed . . . and one, who led the way, was clad in a ghoulishly humped black coat and striped trousers, and had a man's felt hat perched on the shapeless thing that answered for a head. . . .

Scrooge later described their predominant colour as a greyish-green, though they had white bellies. They were mostly shiny and slippery, but the ridges of their backs were scaly. Their forms vaguely suggested the anthropoid, while their heads were the heads of fish, with prodigious bulging eyes that never closed. At the sides of their necks were palpitating gills, and their long paws were webbed. They hopped irregularly, sometimes on two legs and sometimes on four. Scrooge was somehow glad that they had no more than four limbs. Their croaking, baying voices, clearly used for articulate speech, held all the dark shades of expression which their staring faces lacked.

But for all of their monstrousness they were not unfamiliar to him. Scrooge knew too well what they must be - for was not the memory of those creatures laughing at Jacob Marley's side still fresh? They were the blasphemous fish-frogs of the nameless design - living and horrible - and as Scrooge saw them he recalled his first visit of the night. The similar shapes lurking in the Miskatonic River, side by side with Old Jacob. Their number was past guessing. It seemed to Scrooge that there were limitless swarms of them and certainly his momentary glimpse could have shown only the least fraction.

In an instant, Scrooge's attention was diverted from the advancing horrors as he heard a loud crash. He turned towards the young boy, who had been cornered on the precipice, but he was gone.

Scrooge held back a scream and staggered away from the edge of the cliff, too horrified to take a look at what unfortunate mess now littered the rocks below. He steadied himself, unsure whether his legs could further carry him, and began to run, fleeing not from the advancing horror of the Deep Ones, but from his Phantom guide.

Downhill he ran, sticking to coastal paths for fear of entering the city and encountering the blasphemous creatures that had pursued the boy. Onwards, through a gate until he stumbled on an outcrop and rolled to the floor.

Scrooge had stumbled and tripped over a gravestone.

He looked about and the Deep Ones appeared to have gone. He was now alone and the night wore on. He lay still for a moment, catching his breath before picking himself up and creeping around the graveyard, desperately trying to conceal any sound for fear the Phantom may discover him.

But his efforts were in vain, stood before him the shrouded figure was poised next to a gravestone. Scrooge, hoping that his visit with the Phantom was drawing to an end, cautiously approached. The Spirit stood among the graves, and pointed down to one. He advanced towards it trembling. The Phantom was exactly as it had been, but he dreaded that he saw new meaning in its solemn shape.

"Before I draw nearer to that stone to which you point," said Scrooge, "answer me one question. Are these the shadows of the things that Will be, or are they shadows of things that May be, only?"

Still the Ghost pointed downward to the grave by which it stood.

"Men's courses will foreshadow certain ends, to which, if persevered in, they must lead," said Scrooge. "But if the courses be departed from, the ends will change. Say it is thus with what you show me!"

The Spirit was immovable as ever.

"The departure of Jacob Marley and my sister, Fan, from this world need not be in vain. I can prevent further suffering, help souls such as the young boy I have just witnessed, prevent their meddling in such affairs as yours. Is that not so, Spirit? Who's grave is this at which you draw me?"

Scrooge crept towards it, trembling as he went; and following the gruesome finger, read upon the stone of the neglected grave his own name, Ebenezer Scrooge.

"Am I that man who lay upon the slate?" he cried, upon his knees.

The finger pointed from the grave to him, and back again.

"No, Spirit! Oh no, no!"

The finger still was there.

"I drowned? And the relative that drove me to such grief?"

The Phantom need not have spoken.

"My dear nephew, Fred? Another loss? Oh, mercy!"

Had Fred become another sacrifice in the name of Cthulhu? Had he joined his mother and father in the murky depths of Y'ha-nthlei?

"Spirit!" he cried, tight clutching at its robe, "hear me! I am not the man I was. I will not be the man I must have been but for this intercourse. Why show me this, if I am past all hope?"

For the first time the hand appeared to shake.

"Good Spirit," he pursued, as down upon the ground he fell before it: "Your nature intercedes for me, and pities me. Assure me that I yet may change these shadows you have shown me, by an altered life!"

The terrible hand trembled.

"I will honour my family and my friends. I will abandon my research and turn away from the pursuit of lost cities and fearsome gods. I will keep Christmas in my heart, and try to keep it all the year. I will live in the Past, the Present, and the Future. I can change these events and end such needless sacrifices. I will not shut out the lessons you have taught. I may sponge away the writing on this stone and the stones of all else who have fallen because of my actions!"

The Phantom took a deep breath. It was the first sound Scrooge had heard it make, and it spoke. It spoke two, terrifying words in a dark, deep voice; "Cthulhu fhtagn"

Cthulhu Rises!

And as it spoke, the creature's shroud dropped and it began to fly, a gigantic, pale, worm-like horror, which ascended in to the sky towards the stars from which it dwells, towards Xoth, preparing for the return of its mate, for by Scrooge's account the Phantom was none other than Idh-yaa. The star at which it travelled began to burn brightly and Scrooge shielded his eyes as he screamed in terror. Brighter the light grew, warm and inviting and Scrooge fainted in horror.

V

Scrooge was aroused from his deep slumber, cold and wet. Opening his eyes, he found himself lying in the same graveyard in which Idh-yaa had abandoned him. Startled to find himself in such a position, Scrooge bounded to his feet. The gravestone, marked Ebenezer Scrooge, was nowhere to be seen. In fact, Scrooge lay in an open patch of grass. No grave yet lay there.

"I will live in the Past, the Present, and the Future!" Scrooge repeated, as he scrambled across the grass. "Oh Jacob Marley! Heaven, and the Christmas Time be praised for this! I say it on my knees, old Jacob; on my knees!"

He was so fluttered and so glowing with his good intentions that his broken voice would scarcely answer to his call. He had been sobbing violently in his conflict with the Spirit, and his face was wet with tears.

"The grave is not here," cried Scrooge, "The shadows of the things that would have been, may be dispelled. They will be. I know they will! I don't know what to do!" cried Scrooge, laughing and crying in the same breath, "I am as light as a feather, I am as happy as an angel, I am as merry as a school-boy. I am as giddy as a drunken man. A merry Christmas to every-body! A happy New Year to all the world!"

Really, for a man who had been out of practice for so many years, it was a splendid laugh, a most illustrious laugh. The father of a long, long line of brilliant laughs!

"I don't know what day of the month it is!" said Scrooge. "I don't know how long I've been among the Spirits. I don't know anything. I'm quite a baby. Never mind. I don't care. I'd rather be a baby!"

He was checked in his transports by the churches ringing out the lustiest peals he had ever heard. Golden sunlight; Heavenly sky; sweet fresh air; merry bells. Oh, glorious. Glorious!

And he ran.

He ran to the courtyard gates, ran down the paths which had led him from the cliff and found a small boy, in his Sunday clothes, stood staring towards the waves, Devil's Reef visible on the distant horizon.

"You! Boy! What day is this?" shouted Scrooge excitedly.

"Today? It's Christmas Day," the boy replied, without turning to him.

Christmas Day. He hadn't missed it!

"Christmas Day! God Bless Us!" Scrooge exclaimed in delight.

"Cthulhu Bless Us, Everyone." The boy said.

Scrooge stopped, his breath caught in his throat.

The boy, sensing Scrooge's unease pointed out in to the harbour. "Cthulhu Fhtagn!" he stated, and Scrooge noticed the grey, slimy skin on the boy's neck. The blasphemous gills throbbing on the side of the boy's head. Scrooge looked out in to the harbour and saw a single mountain-top, the hideous monolith-crowned citadel whereon great Cthulhu was buried, emerged from the waters.

Christmas Day.

Cthulhu Rises.

Scrooge wanted to run, but found himself unable to muster himself. This was no longer a shadow of things gone or things yet to be.

When I think of the extent of all that may be brooding down there I almost wish to kill myself forthwith. Scrooge was awed by the cosmic majesty of this dripping Babylon of elder daemons, and must have guessed without guidance that it was nothing of this or of any sane planet. Awe at the unbelievable size of the greenish stone blocks, at the dizzying height of the great carven monolith, and at the stupefying identity of the colossal statues and bas-reliefs with the queer image found in the shrine on the Alert, was poignantly visible in every line of Scrooge's frightened description to me.

I asked Scrooge directly for a description of this fascinating sight, and he spoke of broad impressions of vast angles and stone surfaces - surfaces too great to belong to anything right or proper for this earth, and impious with horrible images and hieroglyphs.

Scrooge knew what he must do to end this terrible nightmare, and so he clambered down the rocky outcrop of the cliff face and waded out in to the water. He took a few final gulps of breath before diving in to the frothy depths of the water and swam towards the cavernous alien outcrop.

How long this took, Scrooge did not tell, but the ominous mountain grew ever nearer until Scrooge could grasp the mud-bank of the monstrous Acropolis, and clambered slipperily up over titan oozy blocks which could have been no mortal staircase. The very sun of heaven seemed distorted when viewed through the polarising miasma welling out from this sea-soaked perversion, and twisted menace and suspense lurked leeringly in those crazily elusive angles of carven rock where a second glance showed concavity after the first showed convexity.

Scrooge climbed up the foot of the monolith and looked curiously at the immense carved door with the squid-dragon bas-relief. It was like a great barn-door; and Scrooge felt that it was a door because of the ornate lintel, threshold, and jambs around it, though he could not decide whether it lay flat like a trap-door or slantwise like an outside cellar-door. As Jacob Marley may have said, had he been present, the geometry of the place was all wrong. One could not be sure that the sea and the ground were horizontal, hence the relative position of everything else seemed phantasmally variable.

Without a touch, the door slid open and Scrooge stared into the aperture, a darkness almost material.

The odour rising from the newly opened depths was intolerable, and at length Scrooge thought he heard a nasty, slopping sound down there. Scrooge listened intently as It lumbered slobberingly into sight and gropingly squeezed Its gelatinous green immensity through the black doorway into the tainted outside air of that poison city of madness.

After vigintillions of years great Cthulhu was loose again, and ravening for delight on Christmas Day.

Scrooge stood silently, arms outstretched, eyes closed as the flabby claws grabbed him. This titan Thing from the stars slavered and gibbered as he took Ebenezer Scrooge into his tentacles. Then, bolder than the storied Cyclops, great Cthulhu slid greasily back into the great city. The doors closed, the city did sink and the people of Innsmouth did sing carols and make merry this Christmas Day.

VI

Miskatonic University declared Ebenezer Scrooge lost at sea. They claim that a madness had taken him and, consumed with ever growing grief for Jacob and Fan, Scrooge travelled to Innsmouth and took his own life. Though his body was never recovered, an empty grave sits in the courtyard on the clifftop of Innsmouth. Locals tell tales of ghostly visitors, grey and slick, who mourn at his graveside every Christmas Eve.

Christmas Day 1928 passed uneventfully for the rest of the World. Revellers made merry and attributed their festive cheer to the Holy Spirit. The sacrifice of Ebenezer Scrooge and the satiated waking of great Cthulhu will no doubt be dismissed.

No doubt you enquire as to how I came by these accounts, for although Scrooge's journal provided much for this tale, there are many details which have yet to be documented by credible witnesses, save one; Ebenezer Scrooge, himself.

Indeed, just as Scrooge had trembled at the first sight of Jacob Marley that Christmas Eve, so did I quake with fear when Scrooge first approached me. It seems his sacrifice to the great Cthulhu did not result in death, but in his conversion to a Deep One also. Ebenezer still relents his time upon the earth, attending his own graveside yearly with Old Jacob and Dear Fan. And still, he fights to end the curse which prevails over his family. Whilst Scrooge's death dissuaded the research of his nephew Fred, a great foreboding still hangs over the family of Ebenezer Scrooge, which with my help Scrooge intends to remedy.

My time on this earth is now short. Scrooge's visits to my window grow less frequent and as winter presses on, I prepare for the day on which my sacrifice to Great Old Ones shall save this planet from Christmas destruction at the hands of restless gods. Miskatonic does not approve my research, cancelling all funding after Scrooge's 'madness', yet my father brought Scrooge's books home and we began to work on maps and tomes together. It was a delightful project for my father and I, his crippled son, to begin together – even if it resulted in his own death.

Last night, I visited the grave of my father, Mr Robert Cratchit, for the last time. I will soon join him and my brothers and sisters in the great city of Y'ha-nthlei – should the great Cthulhu show me mercy.

My account of the true mysteries of Christmas will no doubt be confiscated by Miskatonic and destroyed. It is my sole hope that another may read this journal before its destruction. Be warned, the path to The Old Ones is treacherous, but necessary to save Christmas for Earth's many joyous inhabitants.

I can only pray you are up to the task.

The Haunted Man And The Reanimator's Bargain

By David Griffiths

I

Everybody said so.

Far be it from me to assert that what everybody says must be true. Everybody is, often, as likely to be wrong as right. In the general experience, everybody has been wrong so often, and it has taken, in most instances, such a weary while to find out how wrong, that the authority is proved to be fallible. Everybody may sometimes be right, but that in itself is no rule.

Yet, everybody said he looked like a haunted man. The extent of my present claim for everybody is, that they were so far right. He did.

Who could have seen his hollow cheek; his sunken brilliant eye; his black-attired figure, indefinably grim, although well-knit and well-proportioned; his grizzled hair hanging, like tangled sea-weed, about his face, - as if he had been, through his whole life, a lonely mark for the chafing and beating of the great deep of humanity, - but might have said he looked like a haunted man?

Who could have observed his manner, taciturn, thoughtful, gloomy, shadowed by habitual reserve, retiring always and jocund never, with a distraught air of reverting to a bygone place and time, or of listening to some old echoes in his mind, but might have said it was the manner of a haunted man?

Who could have heard his voice, slow-speaking, deep, and grave, with a natural fullness and melody in it which he seemed to set himself against and stop, but might have said it was the voice of a haunted man?

Who that had seen him in his inner chamber, part library and part laboratory, - for he was, as the world knew, far and wide, a learned man of medicine, and a teacher on whose lips and hands a crowd of aspiring ears and eyes hung daily, - who that had seen him there, upon a winter night, alone, surrounded by his drugs and instruments and books; the shadow of his shaded lamp a monstrous beetle on the wall, motionless among a crowd of spectral shapes raised there by the flickering of the fire upon the quaint objects around him - who that had seen him then, his work done, and he pondering in his chair before the rusted grate and red flame, moving his thin mouth as if in speech, but silent as the dead, would not have said that the man seemed haunted and the chamber too?

Who might not, by a very easy flight of fancy, have believed that everything about him took this haunted tone, and that he lived on haunted ground?

There was one who may have argued that the man was not haunted. His name was Herbert West, a friend and colleague of mine whom I have spoken of before my confinement in this sanatorium. Of his death and his vile experiments, to which I was a willing party, I have previously elaborated. But of his relationship to the Haunted Man, I will now discuss. Most will think me mad, that my tale is brought about from my condition. But West is now gone, torn apart by his monstrous creations, and as his spell upon me falters, my recollection of events becomes clearer.

But first, the Haunted Man. His dwelling was so solitary and vault-like, - an old, retired part of an ancient endowment for students at Miskatonic, once a brave edifice, planted in an open place, but now the obsolete whim of forgotten architects; smoke-age-and-weather-darkened, squeezed on every side by the overgrowing of the great city, and choked, like an old well, with stones and bricks; its small quadrangles, lying down in very pits formed by the streets and buildings, which, in course of time, had been constructed above its heavy chimney stalks; its old trees, insulted by the neighbouring smoke, which deigned to droop so low when it was very feeble and the weather very moody; its grass-plots, struggling with the mildewed earth to be grass, or to win any show of compromise; its silent pavements, unaccustomed to the tread of feet, and even to the observation of eyes, except when a stray face looked down from the upper world, wondering what nook it was; its sun-dial in a little bricked-up corner, where no sun had straggled for a hundred years, but where, in compensation for the sun's neglect, the snow would lie for weeks when it lay nowhere else, and the black east wind would spin like a huge humming-top, when in all other places it was silent and still.

His dwelling, at its heart and core - within doors - at his fireside - was so lowering and old, so crazy, yet so strong, with its worn-eaten beams of wood in the ceiling, and its sturdy floor shelving downward to the great oak chimney-piece; so environed and hemmed in by the pressure of the town yet so remote in fashion, age, and custom; so quiet, yet so thundering with echoes when a distant voice was raised or a door was shut, - echoes, not confined to the many low passages and empty rooms, but rumbling and grumbling till they were stifled in the heavy air of the forgotten Crypt, half-buried in the earth. The Crypt in which he would conduct his most secretive of experiments and in which Herbert West was once a temporary resident.

You should have seen him in his dwelling about twilight, in the dead winter time. When he sat gazing at the fire. When, as it rose and fell, the shadows went and came. When he took no heed of them, with his bodily eyes; but, let them come or let them go, looked fixedly at the fire. You should have seen him, then.

When a knock came at his door, in short, as he was sitting so, and roused him.

"Who's that?" he said. "Come in!"

Surely there had been no figure leaning on the back of his chair; no face looking over it. It is certain that no gliding footstep touched the floor, as he lifted up his head, with a start, and spoke. And yet there was no mirror in the room on whose surface his own form could have cast its shadow for a moment; and, Something had passed darkly and gone!

"I'm humbly fearful, sir," said a fresh-coloured busy man, holding the door open with his foot for the admission of himself and a wooden tray he carried, and letting it go again by very gentle and careful degrees, when he and the tray had got in, lest it should close noisily, "that it's a good bit past the time tonight. But Mrs. William has been taken off her legs so often" -

"By the wind? Ay! I have heard it rising."

" - By the wind, sir - that it's a mercy she got home at all. Oh dear, yes. Yes. It was by the wind, Mr. Redlaw. By the wind. Mrs. William is of course subject at any time, sir, to be taken off her balance by the elements. She is not formed superior to that."

"No," returned Mr. Redlaw good-naturedly, though abruptly.

"Mrs. William must be taken out of elements for the strength of her character to come into play. Yes, sir. Oh dear, yes!" said Mr. Swidger, still proceeding with his preparations, and checking them off as he made them. "That's where it is, sir. That's what I always say myself, sir. Such a many of us Swidgers! Why there's my father, sir, superannuated keeper and custodian of this Institution, eighty-seven year old. He's a Swidger!"

"True, William," was the patient and abstracted answer, when he stopped again.

"Yes, sir," said Mr. Swidger. "That's what I always say, sir. You may call him the trunk of the tree! Then you come to his successor, my unworthy self and Mrs. William, Swidgers both. Then you come to all my brothers and their families, Swidgers, man and woman, boy and girl. Why, what with cousins, uncles, aunts, and relationships of this, that, and t'other degree, and whatnot degree, and marriages, and lyings-in, the Swidgers might take hold of hands, and stretch across Massachusetts!"

Receiving no reply at all here, from the thoughtful man whom he addressed, Mr. William approached, him nearer, and made a feint of accidentally knocking the table with a decanter, to rouse him. The moment he succeeded, he went on, as if in great alacrity of acquiescence.

"Yes, sir! That's just what I say myself, sir. Mrs. William and me have often said so. 'There's Swidgers enough,' we say, 'without our voluntary contributions,' In fact, sir, my father is a family in himself to take care of; and it happens all for the best that we have no child of our own, though it's made Mrs. William rather quiet-like, too. Quite ready for the fowl and mashed potatoes, sir? Mrs. William said she'd dish in ten minutes when I left the Lodge."

"I am quite ready," said the other, waking as from a dream, and walking slowly to and fro.

"Mrs. William has been at it again, sir!" said the keeper, as he stood warming a plate at the fire, and pleasantly shading his face with it. Mr. Redlaw stopped in his walking, and an expression of interest appeared in him.

"What I always say myself, sir. She will do it! There's a motherly feeling in Mrs. William's breast that must and will have went."

"What has she done?"

"Why, sir, not satisfied with being a sort of mother to all the young gentlemen that come up from a variety of parts, to attend your courses of lectures at this learned foundation - it's surprising how stone-chaney catches the heat this frosty weather, to be sure!" Here he turned the plate, and cooled his fingers.

"Well?" said Mr. Redlaw.

"That's just what I say myself, sir," returned Mr William, speaking over his shoulder, as if in ready and delighted assent. "That's exactly where it is, sir! There isn't one of our students but appears to regard Mrs William in that light. Every day, right through the course, they put their heads into the Lodge, one after another, and have all got something to tell her, or something to ask her. 'Swidge' is the appellation by which they speak of Mrs William in general, among themselves, I'm told; but that's what I say, sir. Better be called ever so far out of your name, if it's done in real liking, than have it made ever so much of, and not cared about! What's a name for? To know a person by, for sure!"

Mrs William, like Mr William, was a simple, innocent-looking person, in whose smooth cheeks the cheerful red of her husband's official waistcoat was very pleasantly repeated. But whereas Mr William's light hair stood on end all over his head, and seemed to draw his eyes up with it in an excess of bustling readiness for anything, the dark brown hair of Mrs William was carefully smoothed down, and waved away under a trim tidy cap, in the most exact and quiet manner imaginable. Whereas Mr William's very trousers hitched themselves up at the ankles, as if it were not in their iron-grey nature to rest without looking about them, Mrs William's neatly-flowered skirts - red and white, like her own pretty face - were as composed and orderly, as if the very wind that blew so hard out of doors could not disturb one of their folds. Whereas his coat had something of a fly-away and half-off appearance about the collar and breast, her little bodice was so placid and neat, that there should have been protection for her, in it, had she needed any, with the roughest people. Who could have had the heart to make so calm a bosom swell with grief, or throb with fear, or flutter with a thought of shame! To whom would its repose and peace have not appealed against disturbance, like the innocent slumber of a child!

"Punctual, of course, Milly," said her husband, relieving her of the tray, "or it wouldn't be you. Here's Mrs. William, sir! - He looks lonelier than ever to-night," whispering to his wife, as he was taking the tray, "and ghostlier altogether."

Without any show of hurry or noise, or any show of herself even, she was so calm and quiet, Milly set the dishes she had brought upon the table, - Mr William, after much clattering and running about, having only gained possession of a butter-boat of gravy, which he stood ready to serve.

"Another Christmas come, another year gone!" murmured the Redlaw, with a gloomy sigh. "More figures in the lengthening sum of recollection that we work and work at to our torment, till Death idly jumbles all together, and rubs all out. So, Philip!" breaking off, and raising his voice as he addressed the elder Swidger – Mr Williams' father.

"My duty to you, sir," returned the old man. "Should have spoken before, sir, but know your ways, Mr Redlaw - proud to say - and wait till spoke to! Merry Christmas, sir, and Happy New Year, and many of 'em. Have had a pretty many of 'em myself - ha, ha! - and may take the liberty of wishing 'em. I'm eighty-seven!"

"Have you had so many that were merry and happy?" asked Redlaw.

"Ay, sir, ever so many," returned the old man.

"Is his memory impaired with age? It is to be expected now," said Mr Redlaw, turning to the son, and speaking lower.

"Not a morsel of it, sir," replied Mr William. "There never was such a memory as my father's. He's the most wonderful man in the world. He doesn't know what forgetting means. It's the very observation I'm always making to Mrs William, sir, if you'll believe me!"

Mr Swidger, in his polite desire to seem to acquiesce at all events, delivered this as if there were no iota of contradiction in it, and it were all said in unbounded and unqualified assent.

The Chemist pushed his plate away, and, rising from the table, walked across the room to where the old man stood looking at a little sprig of holly in his hand.

"It recalls the time when many of those years were old and new, then?" he said, observing him attentively, and touching him on the shoulder. "Does it?"

"Oh many, many!" said Philip, half awaking from his reverie. "I'm eighty-seven!"

"Merry and happy, was it?" asked the Chemist in a low voice. "Merry and happy, old man?"

"Maybe as high as that, no higher," said the old man, holding out his hand a little way above the level of his knee, and looking retrospectively at his questioner, "when I first remember them! Cold, sunshiny day it was, out a-walking, when some one - it was my mother as sure as you stand there, though I don't know what her blessed face was like, for she took ill and died that Christmas-time - told me they were food for birds. The pretty little fellow thought - that's me, you understand - that birds' eyes were so bright, perhaps, because the berries that they lived on in the winter were so bright. I recollect that."

"Merry and happy!" mused Redlaw, bending his dark eyes upon the stooping figure, with a smile of compassion. "Merry and happy - and remember well?"

"Ay," resumed the old man, catching the last words. "I remember them well in my school time, year after year, and all the merry-making that used to come along with them. I was a strong chap then, Mr. Redlaw."

"That's what I always say, father!" returned the son promptly, and with great respect. "You ARE a Swidger, if ever there was one of the family!"

"Dear!" said the old man, shaking his head as he again looked at the holly. "His mother - my son William's my youngest son - and I, have sat among them all, boys and girls, little children and babies, many a year, when the berries like these were not shining half so bright all round us, as their bright faces. Many of them are gone; she's gone; and my son George (our eldest, who was her pride more than all the rest!) is fallen very low since his sister died, earlier this year. George misses her dearly, as do we all: but I can see them, when I look here, alive and healthy, as they used to be in those days; and I can see him, thank God, in his innocence. It's a blessed thing to me, at eighty-seven."

The keen look that had been fixed upon him with so much earnestness, had gradually sought the ground.

"When my circumstances got to be not so good as formerly, it was quite a pleasure to know that one of our founders - or more correctly speaking," said the old man, with a great glory in his subject and his knowledge of it, "one of the learned gentlemen that helped endow Miskatonic, has a portrait that hangs in the Dinner Hall. A sedate gentleman in a peaked beard, and a scroll below him, in old English letters, 'Lord! keep my memory green!' You know all about him, Mr. Redlaw?"

"I know the portrait hangs there, Philip."

"Yes, sure, it's the second on the right, above the panelling. I was going to say - he has helped to keep my memory green, I thank him; for going round the building every year, as I'm a doing now, and freshening up the bare rooms with these branches and berries, freshens up my bare old brain. One year brings back another, and that year another, and those others numbers! At last, it seems to me as if the birth-time of our Lord was the birth-time of all I have ever had affection for, or mourned for, or delighted in, - and they're a pretty many, for I'm eighty-seven!"

"Merry and happy," murmured Redlaw to himself.

The room began to darken strangely.

"So you see, sir," pursued old Philip, whose hale wintry cheek had warmed into a ruddier glow, and whose blue eyes had brightened while he spoke, "I have plenty to keep, when I keep this present season. Now, where's my quiet Mouse? Chattering's the sin of my time of life, and there's half the building to do yet, if the cold don't freeze us first, or the wind don't blow us away, or the darkness don't swallow us up."

The quiet Mouse had brought her calm face to his side, and silently taken his arm, before he finished speaking.

"Come away, my dear," said the old man. "Mr Redlaw won't settle to his dinner, otherwise, till it's cold as the winter. I hope you'll excuse me rambling on, sir, and I wish you good night, and, once again, a merry - "

"Stay!" said Mr Redlaw, resuming his place at the table, more, it would have seemed from his manner, to reassure the old keeper, than in any remembrance of his own appetite. "Spare me another moment, Philip. William, you were going to tell me something to your excellent wife's honour. It will not be disagreeable to her to hear you praise her. What was it?"

"Why, that's where it is, you see, sir," returned Mr William Swidger, looking towards his wife in considerable embarrassment. "Mrs William's got her eye upon me."

"But you're not afraid of Mrs William's eye?"

"Why, no, sir," returned Mr Swidger, "It wasn't made to be afraid of. It wouldn't have been made so mild, if that was the intention."

Mr William, standing behind the table, and rummaging disconcertedly among the objects upon it, directed persuasive glances at Mrs William, and secret jerks of his head and thumb at Mr Redlaw, as alluring her towards him.

"Down in the Buildings. Tell, my dear! You're the works of Shakespeare in comparison with myself. Down in the Buildings, you know, my love. The Student."

"Student?" repeated Mr Redlaw, raising his head.

"I didn't know," said Milly, with a quiet frankness, free from any haste or confusion, "that William had said anything about it, or I wouldn't have come. I asked him not to. It's a sick young gentleman, sir - and very poor, I am afraid - who is too ill to go home this holiday-time, and lives, unknown to any one, in but a common kind of lodging for a gentleman, down in Jerusalem Buildings. That's all, sir."

"Why have I never heard of him?" said the Chemist, rising hurriedly. "Why has he not made his situation known to me? Sick! - give me my hat and cloak. Poor! - what house? - what number?"

"Oh, you mustn't go there, sir," said Milly, leaving her father-in-law, and calmly confronting him with her collected little face and folded hands.

"Not go there?"

"Oh dear, no!" said Milly, shaking her head as at a most manifest and self-evident impossibility. "It couldn't be thought of!"

"What do you mean? Why not?"

"Why, you see, sir," said Mr William Swidger, persuasively and confidentially, "the young gentleman would never have made his situation known to one of his own sex. Mrs Williams has got into his confidence, but that's quite different. They all confide in Mrs William; they all trust her. A man, sir, couldn't have got a whisper out of him; but woman, sir, and Mrs William combined - !"

"There is good sense and delicacy in what you say, William," returned Mr Redlaw, observant of the gentle and composed face at his shoulder. And laying his finger on his lip, he secretly put his purse into her hand.

"Oh dear no, sir!" cried Milly, giving it back again. "Worse and worse! Couldn't be dreamed of! He said that of all the world he would not be known to you, or receive help from you - though he is a student in your class. I have made no terms of secrecy with you, but I trust to your honour completely."

"Why did he say so?"

"Indeed I can't tell, sir," said Milly, after thinking a little, "because I am not at all clever, you know; and I wanted to be useful to him in making things neat and comfortable about him, and employed myself that way. But I know he is poor, and lonely, and I think he is somehow neglected too."

The room had darkened more and more. There was a very heavy gloom and shadow gathering behind the Chemist's chair.

"What more about him?" he asked.

"He is engaged to be married when he can afford it," said Milly, "and is studying, I think, to qualify himself to earn a living. I have seen, a long time, that he has studied hard and denied himself much. He muttered in his broken sleep yesterday afternoon, after talking to me about someone dead, and some great wrong done that could never be forgotten; but whether to him or to another person, I don't know. Not by him, I am sure."

"And, in short, Mrs William, you see" said Mr. William, coming up to him to speak in his ear, "has done him worlds of good! Bless you, worlds of good!"

The room turned darker and colder, and the gloom and shadow gathering behind the chair was heavier.

"Not content with this, sir, Mrs William goes and finds, this very night, when she was coming home (why it's not above a couple of hours ago), a creature more like a young wild beast than a young child, shivering upon a door-step. What does Mrs William do, but brings it home to dry it, and feed it, and keep it till our old Bounty of food and flannel is given away, on Christmas morning! If it ever felt a fire before, it's as much as ever it did; for it's sitting in the old Lodge chimney, staring at ours as if its ravenous eyes would never shut again. It's sitting there, at least," said Mr William, correcting himself, on reflection, "unless it's bolted!"

"Heaven keep her happy!" said the Chemist aloud, "and you too, Philip! and you, William! I must consider what to do in this. I may desire to see this student, I'll not detain you any longer now. Goodnight!"

As they passed out and shut the heavy door, which, however carefully withheld, fired a long train of thundering reverberations when it shut at last, the room turned darker.

As he fell a musing in his chair alone, the gloom and shadow thickened behind him, in that place where it had been gathering so darkly. Out of it there came a man, who had been listening in the dark shadows of the room for the entire conversation. It was this man who haunted Redlaw. This was his temporary and secret lodger, Herbert West, a small, slender, spectacled youth with delicate features, yellow hair, pale blue eyes, and a soft voice. The dread companion of the haunted man!

At length he spoke; without moving or lifting up his face.

"Here again!" Redlaw said.

"Here again," replied West. "The old man still mourns the passing of his daughter."

"Why should he not? Less than a year has passed. And still, you remain in my home, in my laboratory. If Swidger were to ever suspect what vile experiments were conducted to his poor daughter."

"Should he ever suspect, your role in her demise would no doubt surface."

"I see you in the fire," said the haunted man; "I hear you in music, in the wind, in the dead stillness of the night. Why do you stay and haunt me thus?"

"I come as I am called," replied West.

"No. Unbidden," exclaimed the Chemist.

"Unbidden be it," said West. "It is enough. I am here."

Hitherto the light of the fire had shone on the two faces. But, now, the haunted man turned, suddenly, and stared upon West. An awful survey, in a lonely and remote part of an empty old pile of building, on a winter night, with the loud wind going by upon its journey of mystery - whence or whither, no man knowing since the world began - and the stars, in unimaginable millions, glittering through it, from eternal space, where the world's bulk is as a grain, and its hoary age is infancy.

"Look upon me!" said West. "I am he, neglected in my youth, and miserably poor, who strove and suffered, and still strove and suffered, until I hewed out knowledge from the mine where it was buried, and made rugged steps thereof, for my worn feet to rest and rise on. A man of science, a path of discovery, to prevent the inevitability of death."

"I am that man," returned the Chemist.

West paused, and seemed to tempt and goad him with a look, and with the manner of his speech, and with his smile.

"I am he," pursued West, "who, in this struggle upward, found a friend. I made him - won him - bound him to me! We worked together, side by side. All the love and confidence that in my earlier youth had had no outlet, and found no expression, I bestowed on him."

"Not all," said Redlaw, hoarsely.

"No, not all," returned West. "William's sister."

The haunted man, with his head resting on his hands, replied "Do not speak of her!" West, with an evil smile, drew closer to the chair, and resting his chin upon his folded hands, looking down into Redlaw's face with searching eyes, that seemed instinct with fire, went on:

"Such glimpses of the light of home as you had ever known, had streamed from her. How young she was, how fair, how loving! She came into the darkness of your life, and made it bright."

"I saw her, in the fire, but now. I hear her in music, in the wind, in the dead stillness of the night," returned the haunted man.

"Did you love her?" said West, echoing his contemplative tone. "I think you did, once. I am sure you did. Better had she loved you less - less secretly, less dearly, from the shallower depths of a more divided heart!"

"Let me forget it!" said the Chemist, with an angry motion of his hand. "Let me blot it from my memory!"

West, without stirring, his cruel eyes still fixed upon Redlaw's face, went on:

"A love, as like hers," pursued West, "as your inferior nature might cherish, arose in your own heart. You loved her far too well. But what pictures of the future did you see? Pictures of your own domestic life, in aftertime, with her who was the inspiration of your toil. Pictures of your dearest, made the wife of a friend, on equal terms - for he had some inheritance, you none - pictures of your sobered age and mellowed happiness, and of the golden links, extending back so far, that should bind you, and your children, in a radiant garland," teased West.

"Pictures," said the haunted man, "that were delusions. Why is it my doom to remember them too well!"

"Delusions," echoed West, and glaring on him with his changeless eyes. "For your friend, passing between you and the centre of the system of your hopes and struggles, won her to himself, and shattered your frail universe. William's young sister, doubly dear, doubly devoted, doubly cheerful in your home, lived on to see you famous, and your old ambition so rewarded when its spring was broken, and then - "

"Then died," he interposed. "Died, gentle as ever; and should have remained that way. Dead, gentle and happy."

"But you read of my research, of my serum and sought my wisdom. A fellow man of medicine. A chance to replicate my accomplishments and prevent death. I warned you of its effects, yet you insisted in its use. Had she but remained a delicate flower, well loved and well remembered."

West stopped and watched him silently.

"Remembered!" said the haunted man, after a pause. "Yes. So well remembered, that even now, when years have passed, and nothing is more idle or more visionary to me than the boyish love so long outlived, I think of it with sympathy, as if it were a younger brother's or a son's. Sometimes I even wonder when her heart first inclined to him, and how it had been affected towards me. - Not lightly, once, I think. - But that is nothing. Early unhappiness, a wound from a hand I loved and trusted, and a loss that nothing can replace, outlive such fancies."

"Thus," said West, "You bear within you a Sorrow and a Wrong. Thus you prey upon yourself. Thus, memory is your curse; and, if you could forget your sorrow and your wrong, you would!"

"Mocker!" said the Chemist, leaping up, and making, with a wrathful hand, at the throat of West. "Why have I always that taunt in my ears?"

"Redlaw!" exclaimed West in an awful voice. "Lay a hand on me, and die!"

He stopped midway, as if its words had paralysed him, and stood looking on a large syringe held by West. The contents a glowing green slime West had his arm raised high in warning; and a smile passed over his features, as he reared his dark figure in triumph.

"If you could forget your sorrow and wrong, you would," West repeated.

"If it be an echo of my thoughts – as it clearly is," rejoined the haunted man, "why should I, therefore, be tormented? It is not a selfish thought. I suffer it to range beyond myself. All men and women have their sorrows, - most of them their wrongs; ingratitude, and sordid jealousy, and interest, besetting all degrees of life. Who would not forget their sorrows and their wrongs?"

"Who would not, truly, and be happier and better for it?" said West.

"These revolutions of years, which we commemorate," proceeded Redlaw, "what do they recall? Are there any minds in which they do not re-awaken some sorrow, or some trouble? What is the remembrance of the old man who was here tonight? A tissue of sorrow and trouble. I called upon you originally to help subdue such remembrances. Why suffer from sorrow when the process of loss can be reversed?"

"But common natures," said West, a smile upon his glassy face, "unenlightened minds and ordinary spirits, do not feel or reason on these things like men of higher cultivation and profounder thought, such as us. Why, even the academics of Miskatonic University consider my research to be blasphemous and abhorrent."

"Tempter," answered Redlaw, "whose hollow look and voice I dread more than words can express, and from whom some dim foreshadowing of greater fear is stealing over me while I speak, I hear again an echo of my own mind."

"You would wish reanimation on those who suffer loss?"

"I would wish life free of sorrow and loss upon those who yet live!" Redlaw offered, "If your experiments in reanimation result in such monstrous creations as I have witnessed, why is this not developed to stem the aging of those yet mortal? Should Old Swidger suffer? Should William and Milly suffer any further losses? Together, we can prevent this!"

"I have the power to prevent their deterioration," returned West. "My work has reached a climax for which I require a willing test subject. Say and it is done."

"I tremble with distrust and doubt of you; and the dim fear you cast upon me deepens into a nameless horror I can hardly bear. - I would not deprive myself of any kindly recollection, or any sympathy that is good for me, or others. What shall I lose, if I assent to this? My humanity?"

"No knowledge; no result of study; nothing but the banishment of future grief, for there will be no need to suffer again. I cannot erase the painful recollections from your past. They have been wont to show themselves in the fire, in music, in the wind, in the dead stillness of the night, in the revolving years," returned West, "but assurance of the future is the guarantee by which this serum works."

West then held his peace.

But having stood before him, silent, for a little while, West moved towards the fire; then stopped.

"Decide!" he said, "before the opportunity is lost!"

"A moment! I call Heaven to witness," said the agitated man, "that I have never been a hater of any kind, - never morose, indifferent, or hard, to anything around me. If, living here alone, I have made too much of all that was and might have been, and too little of what is, the evil, I believe, has fallen on me, and not on others. But, if there were poison in my body, should I not, possessed of antidotes and knowledge how to use them, use them?"

"Say," said West, "is it done?"

"A moment longer!" he answered hurriedly. "All human memory is fraught with sorrow and trouble. Yes, I close the bargain. Yes! I WILL forget my sorrow, wrong, and trouble and forge a new path for mankind!"

"You agree?" West asked, brandishing his serum.

"I do!"

"Then take this with you," exclaimed Herbert West as he injected the green, dreadful serum in to Redlaw's veins, "The gift that I have given, you shall give again, go where you will. Without recovering yourself the power that you have yielded up, you shall henceforth destroy death in all whom you approach. Be happy in the good you have won, and in the good you do!"

West, who had resided in the crypt of Redlaw's abode for the better part of a year, now packed swiftly and departed, leaving Redlaw alone and invigorated.

Later that night, as Redlaw sat alone in his study, a shrill cry reached his ears. It came, not from the passages beyond the door, but from another part of the old building, and sounded like the cry of someone in the dark who had lost the way.

He looked confusedly upon his hands and limbs, as if to be assured of his identity, and then shouted in reply, loudly and wildly; for there was a strangeness and terror upon him, as if he too were lost.

The cry responding, and being nearer, he caught up the lamp, and raised a heavy curtain in the wall, by which he was accustomed to pass into and out of the theatre where he lectured, - which adjoined his room. Associated with youth and animation, and a high amphitheatre of faces which his entrance charmed to interest in a moment, it was a ghostly place when all this life was faded out of it, and stared upon him like an emblem of Death.

"Hello!" he cried. "This way! Come to the light!" When, as he held the curtain with one hand, something rushed past him into the room like a wild-cat, and crouched down in a corner.

"What is it?" he said, hastily.

He might have asked "What is it?" even had he seen it well, as presently he did when he stood looking at it gathered up in its corner.

A bundle of tatters, held together by a hand, in size and form almost an infant's, but in its greedy, desperate little clutch, a bad old man's. A face rounded and smoothed by some half-dozen years, but pinched and twisted by the experiences of a life. Bright eyes, but not youthful. Naked feet, beautiful in their childish delicacy, - ugly in the blood and dirt that cracked upon them. A baby savage, a young monster, a child who had never been a child, a creature who might live to take the outward form of man, but who, within, would live and perish a mere beast.

Used, already, to be worried and hunted like a beast, the boy crouched down as he was looked at, and looked back again, and interposed his arm to ward off the expected blow.

"I'll bite," he said, "if you hit me!"

The thought of biting drew Redlaw back to his gruesome experiments with West, of the corpses taken from newly dug graves and the reanimated bodies, wild and frantic, illegible and irrational.

"Where's the woman?" the boy said. "I want to find the woman."

"Who?"

"The woman. Her that brought me here, and set me by the large fire. She was so long gone, that I went to look for her, and lost myself. I don't want you. I want the woman."

He made a spring, so suddenly, to get away, that the dull sound of his naked feet upon the floor was near the curtain, when Redlaw caught him by his rags.

"Come! you let me go!" muttered the boy, struggling, and clenching his teeth. "I've done nothing to you. Let me go, will you, to the woman!"

"What is your name?"

"Got none. You let me go, will you? I want to find the woman."

The Chemist led him to the door. "This way," he said, looking at him still confusedly. "I'll take you to her." As the Chemist, with a dislike to touch him, sternly motioned him to follow, and was going out of the door, he trembled and stopped, remembering the final words of Herbert West before his departure; "The gift that I have given, you shall give again, go where you will!"

West's words seemed to be blowing in the wind, and the wind blew chill upon him. What if West's experiment were to go wrong? Redlaw had been inoculated only hours ago. Would that things go awry and Milly a victim, Redlaw could not forgive himself.

"I'll not go there, tonight," he murmured faintly. "I'll go nowhere tonight. Go straight down this long-arched passage, and past the great dark door into the yard, - you see the fire shining on the window there."

"The woman's fire?" inquired the boy.

He nodded, and the naked feet had sprung away. He came back to his study, locked his door hastily, and sat down in his chair, covering his face like one who was frightened at himself.

For now he was, indeed, alone.

II

A small man sat in a small parlour, partitioned off from a small shop by a small screen, pasted all over with small scraps of newspapers. In company with the small man, was almost any amount of small children you may please to name - at least it seemed so; they made, in that very limited sphere of action, such an imposing effect, in point of numbers.

The small man who sat in the small parlour, making fruitless attempts to read his newspaper peaceably in the midst of this disturbance, was the father of the family, and the chief of the firm described in the inscription over the little shop front, by the name and title of A. TETTERBY AND CO., NEWSMEN.

Tetterby's was the corner shop in Jerusalem Buildings. There was a good show of literature in the window, chiefly consisting of picture-newspapers out of date, and serial pirates, and footpads. Walking-sticks, likewise, and marbles, were included in the stock in trade. It had once extended into the light confectionery line; but it would seem that those elegancies of life were not in demand about Jerusalem Buildings, for nothing connected with that branch of commerce remained in the window, except a sort of small glass jar containing a languishing mass of bull's-eyes, which had melted in the summer and congealed in the winter until all hope of ever getting them out, or of eating them without eating the jar too, was gone for ever. Tetterby's had tried its hand at several things. It had once made a feeble little dart at the toy business; for, in another jar, there was a heap of minute wax dolls, all sticking together upside down, in the direst confusion, with their feet on one another's heads, and a precipitate of broken arms and legs at the bottom. It had made a move in the millinery direction, which a few dry, wiry bonnet-shapes remained in a corner of the window to attest. It had fancied that a living might lie hidden in the tobacco trade, and had stuck up a representation of a native in the act of consuming that fragrant weed; with a poetic legend attached, importing that united in one cause they sat and joked, one chewed tobacco, one took snuff, one smoked: but nothing seemed to have come of it - except flies. Time had been when it had put a forlorn trust in imitative jewellery, for in one pane of glass there was a card of cheap seals, and another of pencil-cases, and a mysterious black amulet of inscrutable intention. But, to that hour, Jerusalem Buildings had bought none of them. In short, Tetterby's had tried so hard to get a livelihood out of Jerusalem Buildings in one way or other, and appeared to have done so indifferently in all, that the best position in the firm was too evidently Co.'s; Co., as a bodiless creation, being untroubled with the vulgar inconveniences of hunger and thirst, being chargeable neither to the poor's-rates nor the assessed taxes, and having no young family to provide for.

Mr Tetterby gave up the perusal of his newspaper as a bad job, and, taking a slow walk across the room, with his hands behind him, and his shoulders raised - his gait according perfectly with the resignation of his manner - addressed himself to his two eldest offspring.

"Your supper will be ready in a minute, 'Dolphus," said Mr Tetterby. "Your mother has been out in the wet, to the cook's shop, to buy it. It was very good of your mother so to do. You shall get some supper too, very soon, Johnny. Your mother's pleased with you, my man, for being so attentive to your precious sister."

As he spoke, the door creaked open and a visitor entered, vailed in a thick, black cloak. Mr Tetterby turned to the pale visitor in the black cloak, who stood still, and whose eyes were bent upon the ground.

"What may be your pleasure, sir," he asked, "with us?"

"I fear that my coming in unperceived," returned the visitor, "has alarmed you; but you were talking and did not hear me. My name is Redlaw. I come from the University hard by. A young gentleman who is a student there, lodges in your house, does he not?"

"Mr Redlaw?" asked Tetterby.

"Yes."

It was a natural action, and so slight as to be hardly noticeable; but the little man, before speaking again, passed his hand across his forehead, and looked quickly round the room, as though he were sensible of some change in its atmosphere. The Chemist, instantly transferring to him the look of dread he had directed towards the wife, stepped back, and his face turned paler.

"The gentleman's room," said Tetterby, "is upstairs, sir. There's a more convenient private entrance; but as you have come in here, it will save your going out into the cold, if you'll take this little staircase and go up to him that way, if you wish to see him."

"Yes, I wish to see him," said the Chemist.

The watchfulness of his haggard look, and the inexplicable distrust that darkened it, seemed to trouble Mr Tetterby. He paused; and looking fixedly at him in return, stood for a minute or so, like a man stupefied, or fascinated.

At length he said, "If you'll follow me."

"No," replied the Chemist, "I don't wish to be attended, or announced to him. He does not expect me. I would rather go alone. I'll find the way."

In the quickness of his expression of this desire, he touched him on the breast. Withdrawing his hand hastily, almost as though he had wounded him by accident (for he did not know in what part of himself his new power resided, or how it was communicated, or how the manner of its reception varied in different persons), he turned and ascended the stair.

But when he reached the top, he stopped and looked down. The wife was standing in the same place, twisting her ring round and round upon her finger. The husband, with his head bent forward on his breast, was musing heavily and sullenly.

The children, still clustering about the mother, gazed timidly after the visitor, and nestled together when they saw him looking down.

"Come!" said the father, roughly. "There's enough of this. Get to bed here!"

The whole brood crept away; little Johnny and the baby lagging last.

The Chemist, paler than before, stole upward like a thief; looking back upon the change below, and dreading equally to go on or return.

"What have I done?" he said, confusedly. "What am I going to do?"

"Be the benefactor of mankind," he thought he heard Herbert West reply.

He looked around, but there was nothing there; and a passage now shutting out the little parlour from his view, he went on, directing his eyes before him at the way he went.

"It is only since last night," he muttered gloomily, "that I have remained shut up, and yet all things are strange to me. I am strange to myself. I am here, as in a dream. What interest have I in this place?"

There was a door before him, and he knocked at it. Being invited, by a voice within, to enter, he complied.

"Is that my kind nurse?" said the voice. "But I need not ask her. There is no one else to come here."

It spoke cheerfully, though in a languid tone, and attracted his attention to a young man lying on a couch, with the back towards the door. He put up his hand as if expecting her to take it, but, being weakened, he lay still, with his face resting on his other hand, and did not turn round.

The Chemist glanced about the room; - at the student's books and papers, piled upon a table in a corner, where they, and his extinguished reading-lamp, now prohibited and put away, told of the attentive hours that had gone before this illness, and perhaps caused it; - at such signs of his old health and freedom, as the out-of-door attire that hung idle on the wall; - at those remembrances of other and less solitary scenes, the little miniatures upon the chimney-piece, and the drawing of home; - at that token of his emulation, perhaps, in some sort, of his personal attachment too, the framed engraving of himself, the looker-on. The time had been, only yesterday, when not one of these objects, in its remotest association of interest with the living figure before him, would have been lost on Redlaw. Now, they were but objects; or, if any gleam of such connexion shot upon him, it perplexed, and not enlightened him, as he stood looking round with a dull wonder.

The student, recalling the thin hand which had remained so long untouched, raised himself on the couch, and turned his head.

"Mr Redlaw!" he exclaimed, and started up.

Redlaw put out his arm.

"Don't come nearer to me. I will sit here. Remain you, where you are!"

He sat down on a chair near the door, and having glanced at the young man standing leaning with his hand upon the couch, spoke with his eyes averted towards the ground.

"I heard, by an accident, by what accident is no matter, that one of my class was ill and solitary. I received no other description of him, than that he lived in this street. Beginning my inquiries at the first house in it, I have found him."

"I have been ill, sir," returned the student, not merely with a modest hesitation, but with a kind of awe of him, "but am greatly better. An attack of fever - of the brain, I believe - has weakened me, but I am much better. I cannot say I have been solitary, in my illness, or I should forget the ministering hand that has been near me."

"You are speaking of the keeper's wife," said Redlaw.

"Yes." The student bent his head, as if he rendered her some silent homage.

"I remembered your name," he said, "when it was mentioned to me down stairs, just now; and I recollect your face. We have held but very little personal communication together?"

"Very little."

"You have retired and withdrawn from me, more than any of the rest, I think?"

The student signified assent.

"And why?" said the Chemist; not with the least expression of interest, but with a moody, wayward kind of curiosity. "Why? How comes it that you have sought to keep especially from me, the knowledge of your remaining here, at this season, when all the rest have dispersed, and of your being ill? I want to know why this is?"

The young man, who had heard him with increasing agitation, raised his downcast eyes to his face, and clasping his hands together, cried with sudden earnestness and with trembling lips:

"Mr Redlaw! You have discovered me. Your concern for your students is widely reported and I am thankful that a teacher such as yourself would fret for my health. I have no doubt, would I have asked, you would have taken me in over Christmas and provided me with warmth and companionship."

"And yet you refuse me?" Redlaw asked.

"I do, sir." The young man replied.

"Why?"

"Because the students of Miskatonic speak of a man who resides with you. A man of unspeakable villainy and blasphemies. His research has seen him expelled from the finest of institutions and now he works in your company. I fear the work in which he involves himself and wish no part in his research."

"I know not of whom you speak," Redlaw said.

"You know not of Herbert West, sir?"

Redlaw stopped.

The student continued, "Better to chance myself upon the kindness of those in the city than be brought before the eye of the Reanimator!"

"Reanimator!" said Redlaw, laughing. "That is what my students call him?"

"So you admit it, sir?"

"I will admit to having harboured the acquaintance of Herbert West, indeed. As of his research, the principles are sound. There are no blasphemies to speak, only science. Let me help you - "

"For Heaven's sake," entreated the shrinking student, "do not let the mere interchange of a few words with me change you like this, sir! Let me pass again from your knowledge and notice. Let me occupy my old reserved and distant place among those whom you instruct. Know me only by the name Hobson.

"Hobson?" pondered Redlaw.

He clasped his head with both his hands, and for a moment turned upon the young man his own intelligent and thoughtful face. But the light passed from it, like the sun-beam of an instant, and it clouded as before.

"The name my mother bears, sir," faltered the young man, "the name she took, when she might, perhaps, have taken one more honoured. Mr Redlaw," hesitating, "I am the child of a marriage that has not proved itself a well-assorted or a happy one. From infancy, I have heard you spoken of with honour and respect - with something that was almost reverence. I have heard of such devotion, of such fortitude and tenderness, of such rising up against the obstacles which press men down, that my fancy, since I learnt my little lesson from my mother, has shed lustre on your name. At last, a poor student myself, from whom could I learn but you?"

Redlaw, unmoved, unchanged, and looking at him with a staring frown, answered by no word or sign.

"I cannot say," pursued the other, "I should try in vain to say, how much it has impressed me, and affected me, to find the gracious traces of the past, in that certain power of winning gratitude and confidence which is associated among us students (among the humblest of us, most) with Mr Redlaw's generous name. Our ages and positions are so different, sir, and I am so accustomed to regard you from a distance, that I wonder at my own presumption when I touch, however lightly, on that theme. But to one who - I may say, who felt no common interest in my mother once - it may be something to hear, now that all is past, with what indescribable feelings of affection I have, in my obscurity, regarded him; with what pain and reluctance I have kept aloof from his encouragement, when a word of it would have made me rich; yet how I have felt it fit that I should hold my course, content to know him, and to be unknown. Mr Redlaw," said the student, faintly, "what I would have said, I have said ill, for my strength is strange to me as yet; but for anything unworthy in this fraud of mine, forgive me, and for all the rest forget me!"

The staring frown remained on Redlaw's face, and yielded to no other expression until the student, with these words, advanced towards him, as if to touch his hand, when he drew back and cried to him:

"Don't come nearer to me!"

The young man stopped, shocked by the eagerness of his recoil, and by the sternness of his repulsion; and he passed his hand, thoughtfully, across his forehead.

"You can yet learn a great deal from me," Redlaw spoke, "I have worked diligently beside Herbert West these past few months and have learnt much. West sought to restore life and was misguided in his attempts. I witnessed his bizarre experiments first hand and I can vouch for the accuracy of his research. However, together we began to pursue a new line of questioning; that of immortality. No longer would humankind perish. We should seek not to reanimate those who have passed beyond this mortal coil. We should relish the opportunity to extend our own mortality permanently."

"Why do you confide in me?" Hobson asked.

"West has departed and I am to continue the work which he has begun. Let me restore your health, give you food and clothing. In return, help me to finish West's experiments."

"I will not."

"There is sorrow and trouble in sickness, is there not?" Redlaw demanded, with a laugh.

The wondering student answered, "Yes."

"In its unrest, in its anxiety, in its suspense, in all its train of physical and mental miseries?" said the Chemist, with a wild unearthly exultation. "All best forgotten, are they not?"

The student, Hobson, did not reply.

"Are humankind to be troubled by such misery in perpetuity? Shall we not enter an age of enlightenment, free of trappings of mortality and guilt-laden sorrows and fears?"

The student did not answer, but again passed his hand, confusedly, across his forehead. Redlaw still held him by the sleeve, when Milly's voice was heard outside.

Redlaw released his hold, as he listened.

"I have feared, from the first moment," he murmured to himself, "to meet her. There is a steady quality of goodness in her, that I dread to influence."

"To what do you refer?" asked Hobson.

"I am a guinea pig. West's greatest experiment. And until our research can be corroborated, I must avoid those who I hold dear. Will you not come with me and help bestow this gift which now flows between us?"

"Gift? What gift have you bestown, sir?"

"Say that you will help me and together we will assure all of our results. Alone, I may be the murderer of what is tenderest and best within her bosom."

She was knocking at the door.

"Shall I dismiss it as an idle foreboding, or still avoid her?" Redlaw muttered, looking uneasily around.

She was knocking at the door again.

"Of all the visitors who could come here," he said, in a hoarse alarmed voice, turning to his companion, "this is the one I should desire most to avoid. Hide me!"

The student opened a frail door in the wall, communicating where the garret-roof began to slope towards the floor, with a small inner room. Redlaw passed in hastily, and shut it after him.

The student then resumed his place upon the couch, and called to her to enter.

"Dear Mr John," said Milly, looking round, "they told me there was a gentleman here."

"There is no one here but I."

"There has been some one?"

"Yes, yes, there has been some one."

She put her little basket on the table, and went up to the back of the couch, as if to take the extended hand - but it was not there. A little surprised, in her quiet way, she leaned over to look at his face, and gently touched him on the brow.

"Are you quite as well to-night? Your head is not so cool as in the afternoon."

"Tut!" said the student, petulantly, "very little ails me."

A little more surprise, but no reproach, was expressed in her face, as she withdrew to the other side of the table, and took a small packet of needlework from her basket. But she laid it down again, on second thoughts, and going noiselessly about the room, set everything exactly in its place, and in the neatest order; even to the cushions on the couch, which she touched with so light a hand, that he hardly seemed to know it, as he lay looking at the fire. When all this was done, and she had swept the hearth, she sat down, in her modest little bonnet, to her work, and was quietly busy on it directly.

He said nothing; but there was something so fretful and impatient in his change of position, that her quick fingers stopped, and she looked at him anxiously.

"The pillows are not comfortable," she said, laying down her work and rising. "I will soon put them right."

"They are very well," he answered. "Leave them alone, pray. You make so much of everything."

"I have been thinking, Mr John, that you have been often thinking of late, when I have been sitting by, how true the saying is, that adversity is a good teacher. Health will be more precious to you, after this illness, than it has ever been. And years hence, when this time of year comes round, and you remember the days when you lay here sick, alone, that the knowledge of your illness might not afflict those who are dearest to you, your home will be doubly dear and doubly blest. Now, isn't that a good, true thing?"

He coldly took a book, and sat down at the table.

She watched him for a little while, until her smile was quite gone, and then, returning to where her basket was, said gently:

"Mr John, would you rather be alone?"

"There is no reason why I should detain you here," he replied.

She made up the little packet again, and put it in her basket. If she had been as passionate as she was quiet, as indignant as she was calm, as angry in her look as she was gentle, as loud of tone as she was low and clear, she might have left no sense of her departure in the room, compared with that which fell upon the lonely student when she went away.

He was gazing drearily upon the place where she had been, when Redlaw came out of his concealment, and came to the door.

"Sickness will not lay its hand on you again," Redlaw exclaimed. "Let us pray, for the time being, your infliction has not spread to dear Milly!"

"What have you done?" returned Hobson. "What change have you wrought in me? What curse have you brought upon me? Give me back myself!"

"A touch, a breath, no matter. The experiment must be deemed a success. Look how healthy you are, already! Come with me to my study, we must record this miracle." Redlaw was almost hysterical.

"Give me back myself!" exclaimed Hobson like a madman. "I am infected! I am infectious! I am charged with poison for my own mind, and the minds of all mankind. You tamper with medicine in the manner of Herbert West. What fate has befallen me! You have cursed me, sir!"

Redlaw wildly hurried out into the night air where the wind was blowing, the snow falling, the cloud-drift sweeping on, the moon dimly shining; and where, blowing in the wind, falling with the snow, drifting with the clouds, shining in the moonlight, and heavily looming in the darkness, were Herbert West's words, "The gift that I have given, you shall give again, go where you will!"

Whither he went, he neither knew nor cared, so that he avoided company. This put it in his mind - he suddenly bethought himself, as he was going along, of the boy who had rushed into his room. And then he recollected that of those with whom he had communicated since West's departure, that boy alone had shown no sign of being changed for the worse.

Were the boy ill? He was but a waif, a wretch. Would he now be restored to health miraculously? Further evidence of West's accomplishment!

And what if the opposite were true? What if the boy were transformed in to a wild and daemonic animal, such as had happened to the sweet daughter of Old Swidger upon her reanimation? If the serum had created the same effects as previously upon the boy, what then?

And what of Redlaw's fate as carrier?

He resolved to trace the boy, for good or for ill. Monstrous and odious as the wild boy may now be, he determined to seek it out, and prove if this were really so; and also to seek it with another intention, which came into his thoughts at the same time.

So, resolving with some difficulty where he was, he directed his steps back to the University campus, and to that part of it where the general porch was, and where, alone, the pavement was worn by the tread of the students' feet.

The keeper's house stood just within the iron gates, forming a part of the chief quadrangle. There was a little cloister outside, and from that sheltered place he knew he could look in at the window of their ordinary room, and see who was within. The iron gates were shut, but his hand was familiar with the fastening, and drawing it back by thrusting in his wrist between the bars, he passed through softly, shut it again, and crept up to the window, crumbling the thin crust of snow with his feet.

The fire, to which he had directed the boy last night, shining brightly through the glass, made an illuminated place upon the ground. Instinctively avoiding this, and going round it, he looked in at the window. At first, he thought that there was no one there, and that the blaze was reddening only the old beams in the ceiling and the dark walls; but peering in more narrowly, he saw the object of his search coiled asleep before it on the floor. He passed quickly to the door, opened it, and went in.

The creature lay in such a fiery heat, that, as the Chemist stooped to rouse him, it scorched his head. So soon as he was touched, the boy, not half awake, clutching his rags together with the instinct of flight upon him, half rolled and half ran into a distant corner of the room, where, heaped upon the ground, he struck his foot out to defend himself.

"Get up!" said the Chemist. "You have not forgotten me?"

The boy stared intently at Redlaw, his breathing rasping. The Chemist's steady eye controlled him somewhat, or inspired him with enough submission to be raised upon his feet, and looked at.

The boy watched his eyes keenly, as if he thought it needful to his own defence, not knowing what he might do next; and Redlaw could see well that no change came over him.

"Where are they?" he inquired.

Again, the boy did not answer. Redlaw grew frustrated.

"Where is the old man with the white hair, and his son?"

But there was no response. The boy simply stared and Redlaw began to fear. "Do you not recognise me? Will you no longer speak? I brought you to this place last night. Answer my questions!"

The boy crept, animal like, towards the roaring fire. Redlaw watched, fascinated, as the boy approached it. He seemingly felt no heat from the raging flames. The room was stifling.

Then, as Redlaw watched on, the boy reached in to the flames. The skin on his arm crackled and his fat spit as his savage little hand moved to pluck the burning coals out of the fire. Redlaw was aghast, stifling his terror as he watched the boy cook painlessly before him.

It chilled his blood to look on the immovable impenetrable thing, in the likeness of a child, with its sharp malignant face turned up to his, and its almost infant hand, ready turning charred and black.

"Listen, boy!" he said. "You must stop this, at once. You have been infected by an experimental solution, a drug designed to negate mortality. It flows within me and I fear its effects upon you are ill. I wish to do you good, not harm. Will you not speak to me? Tell me you understand, show me signs of rational thought, I beg you!"

He made a hasty step towards the door, afraid of what the boy may do next. He could hear the raspy breathing, saw the cold, cloudy eyes glazed in the boy's head. West's formula was a failure. Certainly on one so young. But what of himself? And what would become of Hobson and Milly? He had encountered them not hours ago. If this child were in such a state now, how long must they have remaining?

But before Redlaw could consider a moment more, the boy leaped from the fireplace, brandishing a white hot piece of coal. He thundered towards Redlaw, who darted to one side to avoid the monstrous creature. The boy collided with the door and the coal scorched the paint. Redlaw ran into the kitchen, frantically rummaging for a means to restrain the poor creature and return him to his laboratory to study and cure. The boy followed, scrabbling on all fours towards him, his sharp rotting teeth bared. Redlaw brandished a butcher's knife and warned the young monster away.

"Get back! Stay back!" he cried, but the boy was beyond rationality. Again, he rushed at Redlaw, who raised the knife in defence, plunging it straight through the boy's chest.

Redlaw cried for what he had done, the boy slumped dead against his body, sinking deeper on to the blade and pushing it through his body, piercing the skin of his back. Redlaw steadied himself, fighting against a faint which now befell him.

"What have you done, West?" he asked, to nobody in particular, "How wrong you were to meddle in such affairs as mortality. Now there is more blood on our hands. I, a murderer."

As he spoke, the boy stirred. His head lifted unnaturally and his teeth reached for Redlaw's arm, desperately seeking nourishment on his flesh. Redlaw recoiled quickly, lifting his foot to the boy's shoulder and pulling his arm free of the open chest wound. He pushed the boy backward and he fell to the floor, his breath stopped. Redlaw watched for a moment, then suddenly, as if rising from a deep slumber, the boy sat upright. The hole in his chest was so large as to see right through. It no doubt penetrated the boy's heart. But still , he rose, reanimated and daemonic.

Redlaw scrambled away, pulling a cleaver from the shelving. He watched the creature stagger, undead, towards him. Redlaw closed his eyes, desperate to block out the horrible act he was about to commit. With a deep breath, he charged at the creature, swinging the cleaver down across its head and splitting its skull in two. It fell, lifeless at last, to the floor and Redlaw wept.

After a moments reprieve, Redlaw searched the house, ensuring none were present. Or worse, none had been attacked by this fiend. He found an address for a sanatorium, home to George Swidger – Phillip's son, who had suffered greatly in the aftermath of his mother's death and whose mental health had deteriorated since the loss of his sister. Presuming that he may find the family there, Redlaw quickly fled the house. If Milly was now infected, there was very little time to save what remained of the Swidger family.

Preferring not to depart by the iron gate by which he had entered, where he would be in danger of meeting her whom he so anxiously avoided, the Chemist led the way, through some of those passages among which the boy had lost himself, and by that portion of the building where he lived, to a small door of which he had the key. When he reached the street, he crept stealthily, eager not to encounter anybody else and bring such a terrible curse upon them. Three times, in his progress, the Chemist caught himself in reverie, and shuddered to think of the horror which had been unleashed. It made him cold. Was he now as devoid of conscious as West?

The first occasion was when he crossed an old churchyard, and Redlaw stopped among the graves, utterly at a loss how to connect them with any tender, softening, or consolatory thought.

The second was, when the breaking forth of the moon induced him to look up at the Heavens, where he saw her in her glory, surrounded by a host of stars he still knew by the names and histories which human science has appended to them; but where he saw nothing else he had been wont to see, felt nothing he had been wont to feel, in looking up there, on a bright night.

The third was when he stopped to listen to a plaintive strain of music, but could only hear a tune, made manifest to him by the dry mechanism of the instruments and his own ears, with no address to any mystery within him, without a whisper in it of the past, or of the future, powerless upon him as the sound of last year's running water, or the rushing of last year's wind.

At each of these three times, he saw with horror that, in spite of the vast intellectual distance between them, and their being unlike each other in all physical respects, the blasphemous crimes committed by Herbert West were also his own.

He journeyed on for some time - now through such crowded places, that he often looked over his shoulder to ensure no human being came in to contact with him, until he arrived at a ruinous collection of houses, and he stopped.

The dim light in the doorway illuminated a sign which read "Sefton Sanatorium", a small, dingy hospital, not nearly as big or clinical as Arkham. Windows were grimy and cracked, paint faded and peeling on the walls. The Swidger family were within.

Redlaw looked about him; from the houses to the waste piece of ground on which the houses stood, or rather did not altogether tumble down, unfenced, undrained, unlighted, and bordered by a sluggish ditch; from that, to the sloping line of arches, part of some neighbouring viaduct or bridge with which it was surrounded, and which lessened gradually towards them, until the last but one was a mere kennel for a dog, the last a plundered little heap of bricks.

Would they let Redlaw in? He pondered on this, briefly, deciding to identify himself as a doctor, for there were many ill inside.

"Sorrow, wrong, and trouble," said the Chemist, with a painful effort at some more distinct remembrance, "at least haunt this place darkly."

There was a woman sitting on the stairs, either asleep or forlorn, whose head was bent down on her hands and knees. As it was not easy to pass without treading on her, and as she was perfectly regardless of his near approach, he stopped, and touched her on the shoulder. Looking up, she showed him quite a young face, but one whose bloom and promise were all swept away, as if the haggard winter should unnaturally kill the spring.

With little or no show of concern on his account, she moved nearer to the wall to leave him a wider passage. Redlaw suddenly sensed dread. Was she yet another forlorn spirit, bereft of death like the boy?

"What are you?" said Redlaw, pausing, with his hand upon the broken stair-rail.

"What do you think I am?" she answered, showing him her face again.

He looked upon the ruined Temple of God, so lately made, so soon disfigured; and something, which was not compassion - for the springs in which a true compassion for such miseries has its rise, were dried up in his breast - but which was nearer to it, for the moment, than any feeling that had lately struggled into the darkening, but not yet wholly darkened, night of his mind - mingled a touch of softness with his next words.

"I am come here to give relief, if I can," he said. "Are you thinking of any wrong?"

She frowned at him, and then laughed; and then her laugh prolonged itself into a shivering sigh, as she dropped her head again, and hid her fingers in her hair.

"Are you thinking of a wrong?" he asked once more.

"I am thinking of my life," she said, with a monetary look at him.

He had a perception that she was one of many, and that he saw the type of thousands, when he saw her, drooping at his feet.

"What are your parents?" he demanded.

"I had a good home once. My father was a gardener, far away, in the country."

"Is he dead?"

"He's dead to me. All such things are dead to me. You a gentleman, and not know that!" She raised her eyes again, and laughed at him.

"Girl!" said Redlaw, sternly, "before this death, of all such things, was brought about, was there no wrong done to you? In spite of all that you can do, does no remembrance of wrong cleave to you? Are there not times upon times when it is misery to you?"

So little of what was womanly was left in her appearance, that now, when she burst into tears, he stood amazed. But he was more amazed, and much disquieted, to note that in her awakened recollection of this wrong, the first trace of her old humanity and frozen tenderness appeared to show itself.

He drew a little off, and in doing so, observed that her arms were black, her face cut, and her bosom bruised.

"What brutal hand has hurt you so?" he asked.

"My own. I did it myself!" she answered quickly.

"It is impossible."

"I'll swear I did! He didn't touch me. I did it to myself in a passion, and threw myself down here. He wasn't near me. He never laid a hand upon me!"

In the white determination of her face, confronting him with this untruth, he saw enough of the last perversion and distortion of good surviving in that miserable breast, to be stricken with remorse that he had ever come near her.

"Sorrow, wrong, and trouble!" he muttered, turning his fearful gaze away. "Would you seek release?"

"I would," she replied.

"I think not," Redlaw replied, "For our time upon this Earth is brief. We must do what we can and treasure our memories – be they good or ill."

"Would that my mother still lived," she sobbed, "my present condition would be much improved?"

"We cannot lament for too long on those gone. If they were to last forever, we should never appreciate them at all. We would become soulless, careless, abhorrent."

Afraid to look at her again, afraid to touch her, afraid to think of having sundered the last thread by which she held upon the mercy of Heaven, he gathered his cloak about him, and glided swiftly up the stairs.

Opposite to him, on the landing, was a door, which stood partly open, and which, as he ascended, a man came forward from within. But this man, on seeing him, drew back, with much emotion in his manner, and, as if by a sudden impulse, mentioned his name aloud.

In the surprise of such a recognition there, he stopped, endeavouring to recollect the wan and startled face. He had no time to consider it, for, to his yet greater amazement, old Philip came out of the room, and took him by the hand. With these words, he pushed the yielding door, and went in.

"Mr Redlaw," said the old man, "this is like you, this is like you, sir! You have heard of it, and have come after us to render any help you can. Ah, too late, too late!"

Redlaw, with a bewildered look, submitted to be led into the room. A man lay there, on a truckle-bed, and William Swidger stood at the bedside.

"Too late!" murmured the old man, looking wistfully into the Chemist's face; and the tears stole down his cheeks.

"That's what I say, father," interposed his son in a low voice. "That's where it is, exactly. To keep as quiet as ever we can while he's a dozing, is the only thing to do. You're right, father!"

Redlaw paused at the bedside, and looked down on the figure that was stretched upon the mattress. It was that of a man, who should have been in the vigour of his life, but on whom it was not likely the sun would ever shine again. The vices of his forty or fifty years' career had so branded him, that, in comparison with their effects upon his face, the heavy hand of Time upon the old man's face who watched him had been merciful and beautifying.

"Who is this?" asked the Chemist, looking round.

"My son George, Mr Redlaw," said the old man, wringing his hands. "My eldest son, George, who was more his mother's pride than all the rest!"

Redlaw's eyes wandered from the old man's grey head, as he laid it down upon the bed, to the person who had recognised him, and who had kept aloof, in the remotest corner of the room. He seemed to be about his own age; and although he knew no such hopeless decay and broken man as he appeared to be, there was something in the turn of his figure, as he stood with his back towards him, and now went out at the door, that made him pass his hand uneasily across his brow.

"William," Redlaw commanded, "there is very little time. I fear I have done your family wrong. I must speak to Milly. The boy, who…"

"William," George said in a gloomy whisper, "who is that man?"

Redlaw looked up, at these words, and, recalling where he was and with whom, and the spell he carried with him - which his surprise had obscured - retired a little, hurriedly, debating with himself whether to shun the house that moment, or remain.

Yielding to a certain sullen doggedness, which it seemed to be a part of his condition to struggle with, he argued for remaining.

"Was it only yesterday," Redlaw thought, "when I observed the memory of this old man to be a tissue of sorrow and trouble, and shall I be afraid, tonight, to shake it? Are such remembrances as I can drive away, so precious to this dying man that I need fear for him? No! I'll stay here."

But he stayed in fear and trembling none the less for these words; and, shrouded in his black cloak with his face turned from them, stood away from the bedside, listening to what they said, as if he felt himself a demon in the place.

"Father!" murmured the sick man, rallying a little from stupor.

"My boy! My son George!" said old Philip.

"You spoke, just now, of my being mother's favourite, long ago. It's a dreadful thing to think now, of long ago!"

"No, no, no;" returned the old man. "Think of it. Don't say it's dreadful. It's not dreadful to me, my son."

"It cuts you to the heart, father." For the old man's tears were falling on him.

"Yes, yes," said Philip, "so it does; but it does me good. It's a heavy sorrow to think of that time, but it does me good, George. Oh, think of it too, think of it too, and your heart will be softened more and more! Where's my son William? William, my boy, your mother loved him dearly to the last, and with her latest breath said, 'Tell him I forgave him, blessed him, and prayed for him.' Those were her words to me. I have never forgotten them, and I'm eighty-seven!"

"Father!" said the man upon the bed, "I am dying, I know. I am so far gone, that I can hardly speak, even of what my mind most runs on. Is there any hope for me beyond this bed?"

"There is hope," returned the old man, "for all who are softened and penitent. There is hope for all such. Oh!" he exclaimed, clasping his hands and looking up, "I was thankful, only yesterday, that I could remember this unhappy son when he was an innocent child, playing happily with his dear sister, now departed."

Redlaw spread his hands upon his face, and shrank, like a murderer.

"Ah!" feebly moaned the man upon the bed. "The waste since then, the waste of life since then!"

"But he was a child once," said the old man. "He played with children. Before he lay down on his bed at night, and fell into his guiltless rest, he said his prayers at his poor mother's knee. I have seen him do it, many a time; and seen her lay his head upon her breast, and kiss him. Sorrowful as it was to her and me, to think of this, when he went so wrong, and when our hopes and plans for him were all broken, this gave him still a hold upon us, that nothing else could have given. Oh, Father, so much better than the fathers upon earth! Oh, Father, so much more afflicted by the errors of Thy children! take this wanderer back! Not as he is, but as he was then, let him cry to Thee, as he has so often seemed to cry to us!"

As the old man lifted up his trembling hands, the son, for whom he made the supplication, laid his sinking head against him for support and comfort, as if he were indeed the child of whom he spoke.

When did man ever tremble, as Redlaw trembled, in the silence that ensued! He knew it must come upon them, knew that it was coming fast.

"My time is very short, my breath is shorter," said the sick man, supporting himself on one arm, and with the other groping in the air, "and I remember there is something on my mind concerning the man who was here just now, Father and William - wait! - is there really anything in black, out there?"

"Yes, yes, it is real," said his aged father.

"Is it a man?"

"What I say myself, George," interposed his brother, bending kindly over him. "It's Mr Redlaw."

"I thought I had dreamed of him. Ask him to come here."

The Chemist, whiter than the dying man, appeared before him. Obedient to the motion of his hand, he sat upon the bed.

"It has been so ripped up, tonight, sir," said the sick man, laying his hand upon his heart, with a look in which the mute, imploring agony of his condition was concentrated, "by the sight of my poor old father, and the thought of all the trouble I have been the cause of, and all the wrong and sorrow lying at my door, that - "

Was it the extremity to which he had come, or was it the dawning of another change, that made him stop?

" - that what I can do right, with my mind running on so much, so fast, I'll try to do. There was another man here. Did you see him?"

Redlaw could not reply by any word; for when he saw that fatal sign he knew so well now, of the wandering hand upon the forehead, his voice died at his lips. But he made some indication of assent.

"He is a small, slender, spectacled with delicate features, yellow hair, pale blue eyes, and a soft yet commanding voice. You know of him, surely."

Redlaw stuttered. "You speak of a colleague of mine, sir."

"Indeed, sir. I do. He has stayed at your lodgings many a night this past year. Is that not so?"

"He has visited," Redlaw said.

It was on his face. His face was changing, hardening, deepening in all its shades, and losing all its sorrow. Death had crept across George Swidger and been left wanting.

"Don't you remember? Don't you know him?" he pursued. "What was his name?"

Redlaw spoke. "Herbert West."

"Murderer!" George shouted, "Liar! Murderer!"

William and Philip rushed to the bedside to console and restrain George. "There, there, George," his brother spoke, "what has come over you? Mr Redlaw is here to help."

"I saw them. Our dear sister was dragged from her grave and taken to their awful laboratory. I saw them! I saw!"

Redlaw went cold and speechless.

"He loved her," George shouted, "and he pined for her. So, Heaven forbid, he stole her corpse and engaged in unholy experiments. They brought her back! Reanimated! The stories of Herbert West are true, father. He is a monster! And Redlaw is no different, for he aided his ghastly research!"

"He is delirious," Redlaw attempted, but he knew George's story to be true. He was a monster, an aberration for aiding such a man as West.

He shut his face out for a moment, with the hand that again wandered over his forehead, and then it lowered on Redlaw, reckless, ruffianly, and callous.

"Why, damn you!" he said, scowling round, "why did you desecrate the grave of my beloved sister? Have you come to do the same to me? What have you been doing to me here? I have lived bold, and I mean to die bold. To the Devil with you!"

And so lay down upon his bed, and put his arms up, over his head and ears, as resolute from that time to keep out all access, and to die in his indifference.

If Redlaw had been struck by lightning, it could not have struck him from the bedside with a more tremendous shock. But the old man, who had left the bed while his son was speaking to him, now returning, avoided it quickly likewise, and with abhorrence.

"Where's my boy William?" said the old man hurriedly. "William, come away from here. We'll go home."

"We should not leave him in such delirium," William told his father, then turned to Redlaw, "Is there nothing that can be done for him?"

Redlaw did not respond.

"Mr Redlaw, my apologies if my brother causes you offence. No harm is meant, sir. He is sick. Why, look at the fever which burns upon his brow." William Swidger lifted his hand to mop his brother's brow. As he did so, George sat bolt upright and sunk his teeth in to William's hand. William let out a scream as George tore two of his fingers from their sockets, blood pouring down his chin as though it were the remnants of some fruit. Philip stood horrified, Redlaw made to restrain George.

He grabbed him by the shoulders and forced him down upon the bed, teeth gnashing, desperately trying to tear more flesh from the bodies of all present. William became faint, falling in to a chair in which his father tended to him.

Redlaw gazed in to the cold eyes of George Swidger, no longer a man. The eyes were clouded and fierce, a great fever had taken him and he licked his lips delightedly, mopping the remnants of his brothers blood, the rest of which had joined the missing appendages in George's stomach. He growled and struggled, but Redlaw held firm.

"Philip!" Redlaw shouted, "You must find a means to subdue him! Quickly!"

"But William..." started Philip, fragile and suddenly very old.

"It is too late!" Redlaw cried, "Help subdue George before we are awash with this plague and we will both undoubtedly perish!"

Philip's eyes darted around the small room, fruitlessly. "I shall get help!" He muttered, and made swiftly for the door. But William had now staggered to his feet and had blocked the doorway unknowingly, steadying himself against the doorframe.

"Quickly!" Redlaw cried, frantically losing his grip upon the monster that clawed at him from the bed.

Philip moved towards the door and William raised his head. Gone now were his pupils and he gazed at his father with the same frosted stare his brother gave Redlaw. He lunged, grabbing his father by his fragile skull and dragged him towards his mouth. There was a sickening pop as Philip's nose was torn from his face. He recoiled screaming as his son advanced toward him, chewing the cartilage between his teeth.

Sensing no escape, Philip clambered toward the window, trying desperately to open it. But William was upon him, pouncing upon his father's back from behind as he tried to tear a piece from his shoulder. His forward momentum brought his dear father off his balance and he tumbled forward. William kept his desperate grip upon his prey as his father crashed through the window, toppling to the street below. Redlaw watched both men disappear and heard a loud crack as they both hit the pavement below, impacting their skulls simultaneously.

Redlaw broke free of George's grip and ran toward the window, but George frantically grabbed at all that he could hold. He rolled from his bed to the floor and caught the trouser leg of Redlaw, who tripped and winded himself with the impact of the hard wooden floor.

Redlaw rolled over, desperately gasping for breath and kicking frantically at George, who was now attempting to climb upon Redlaw and restrain him as though he were the prey of some carnivorous animal. Unable to stand, Redlaw scrambled backwards across the floor, shuffling ever nearer to the window. George pursued, gurgling and groaning as if possessed by some evil spirit. Redlaw reached his hand up to the window and snapped a shard of glass from the broken pane.

As Redlaw fumbled, distractedly, the creature that was once George sensed his opening, and threw himself at Redlaw, who turned, with broken window pane in hand, and thrust it deep inside the skull of George, who stopped immediately. He convulsed suddenly as what remained of his life was stolen away from him, then slumped backwards and lay in an expanding pool of his own blood.

Redlaw gasped and cried. He sat staring at the body of George, deep in horrific thought. When he tried to rise, his legs would barely support him. He steadied himself on the window ledge and looked out at the expansive mess of bodies on the pavement below. All but Milly were now dead, victims of the vile formula designed by Herbert West, with the full cooperation of Redlaw himself.

He must destroy any remnants of those vile experimentations. Redlaw thought of the remnants of spent vials, sat in his laboratory in the crypt. He must take them and burn them. He must ensure no other human being is subjected to such a plague as this. Were this to be unleashed upon the whole of Arkham, what then? How long would such an infection take to spread across Massachusetts? And then, how long to the wider United States, and ultimately its neighbouring continents?

A terror then struck Redlaw, as he thought of the one other whom he had contacted since his gift was bestowed. The young student, Hobson, whom he had cured earlier this very night. What of the Tetterby's, who cared for the sickly student? When last Redlaw spoke to the boy, he was coherent, if perturbed by Redlaw's meddling with West.

Redlaw decided that he must visit Tetterby's and determine the fate of the student, Hobson. Perhaps a scientific mind such as his would maintain rationality and not descend in to the madness that had infected the rest of the subjects. And if Hobson's blood still proved pure, perhaps Redlaw could save both himself and Milly before it was too late.

He rushed down the snow-covered streets surrounding Miskatonic, keeping to shadows and alleyways as best he could, until he reached Tetterby's shop.

It appeared, at first glance, to be closed. This would not appear unusual to any passers-by, for the shop mainly serviced the University campus and being Christmas time most of the academia had returned home to family. Perhaps they had decided to close early?

Redlaw attempted to gaze through the grimy window, but the shop was in darkness. He reached for the door handle, which opened without struggle. Cautiously, he stepped inside.

The shop was silent, a marked difference compared to the bustle earlier in the day. Tetterby lived here with his large family, surely there would be somebody present? He crept through to the parlour, whispering, "Hello? Tetterby?" He reached feebly for a light switch, hoping to see more than just shadows around the room. He caught the switch on the wall and flicked it.

The sight which greeted him was one of unspeakable horror.

He rushed from the room, retching at the sight of the gnarled pile of fresh carcasses that had been deposited in the parlour. In the light, he could see the stains of blood upon the carpets and the walls. There had been a struggle, one which the Tetterby family had lost and paid for with their lives. Their bodies had been stripped of meat, the children moreso that the adult family members. The bodies of the children had been stripped to the bone, as if they were a Christmas goose. Redlaw knew these ghoulish images would remain with him for the rest of his days.

Redlaw, on regaining his composure, noticed a trail of blood, as if a carcass had been dragged across the floor. It led around the counter of the shop and up the stairs. Taking a deep breath, Redlaw slowly crept after the trail, following it up the stairs, desperately avoiding creaks in the boards.

As he reached the top of the stairs, he could hear the rasp of breathing, similar to that which he had heard from the young boy back at the Swidger lodging. He crept towards Hobson's bedroom and slowly pressed his ear to the door. He could hear breathing. Somebody, something was alive, or as alive as might be, and sat in the room.

Redlaw slowly turned the doorknob, pausing momentarily as the bolt clicked out of its mooring. Silently, he pulled the door open and crack and peered in.

Sat upon the bed, was the student, Hobson. His stomach was gorged, as if he had eaten ten Christmas dinners all at once. He held something in his hand, which Redlaw could not identify at the angle at which he leered. Hobson's bedclothes were stained with a deep, crimson, his hands were awash with it and his face just as hewn. Slowly, he lifted the thing in his hand and examined it, as if to find the juiciest morsel of which to take a bite. After a period of close scrutiny, he drew it close with both hands and ripped a stringy piece of meat free with his teeth.

As he did this, Redlaw realised to his horror what Hobson held. It was an adult foot, torn off from the ankle.

Gasping in horror at such knowing cannibalism, Redlaw choked his breath back, which drew the attention of the student. He turned towards the door, dropping the severed foot on to the mattress and slowly rising as if from a deep slumber. He paced towards the door and Redlaw turned to flee. He ran for the stairs, but Hobson lunged out of the door and grabbed at him whilst he ran. Redlaw averted Hobson's grasp and continued to hurtle down the stairs, but Hobson's momentum propelled him over the bannister.

Redlaw cleared the stairwell just in time, as Hobson's body tumbled down the bloodied stairs, landing in a heap on the floor. Was he still alive? Redlaw was terrified to approach, and so he waited. Within minutes, he could hear the rasp of breath, but the creature struggled to move, seemingly having damaged its spinal column in the fall.

Redlaw, leaving the crippled monstrosity at the base of the stairs, searched the house for some rope, whilst desperately trying to avoid sight of the hideous deeds which had taken place in the parlour at Hobson's hands. Finding some rope and a large wheelbarrow, he bound and gagged the creature and placed it in to the makeshift transportation. He covered it with some muslin and quickly pushed him back to his lodgings at Miskatonic.

For a short distance Hobson groaned and attempted to thrash; but their return was more like a flight than a walk, with the Chemist's rapid strides. Shrinking from any remnants of daylight, shrouded in his cloak driving the wheelbarrow as fast as it could, and keeping the cloak drawn closely about him, as though there were mortal contagion in any fluttering touch of his garments, he made no pause until they reached the door by which he had come out. He unlocked it with his key, went in, accompanied by the restrained student, and hastened through the dark passages to his own laboratory.

He carried the remains of his student down to the laboratory and secured him to a large table. The creature still gnarled and gnashed at him, but seemingly no longer had control of its central nervous system. Its constantly thrashing jaw was all it seemed capable of moving.

Redlaw took a blood sample and placed it under a microscope. Should he be able to discover the deficiency in this poor student, he may yet hope to save himself and Milly.

Milly!

The very thought of the girl made him weep. Her family was now gone, turned to ravenous, carnivorous monsters. The Tetterby's were also dead, a mountain of bones left piled in their own parlour.

The key to saving her, if it could be so, lay tethered to his laboratory table and for the remainder of the night, Redlaw turned his full attention to its study.

How long it was before he was aroused from his contemplation of this creature, whom he dreaded so - whether half-an-hour, or half the night - he knew not.

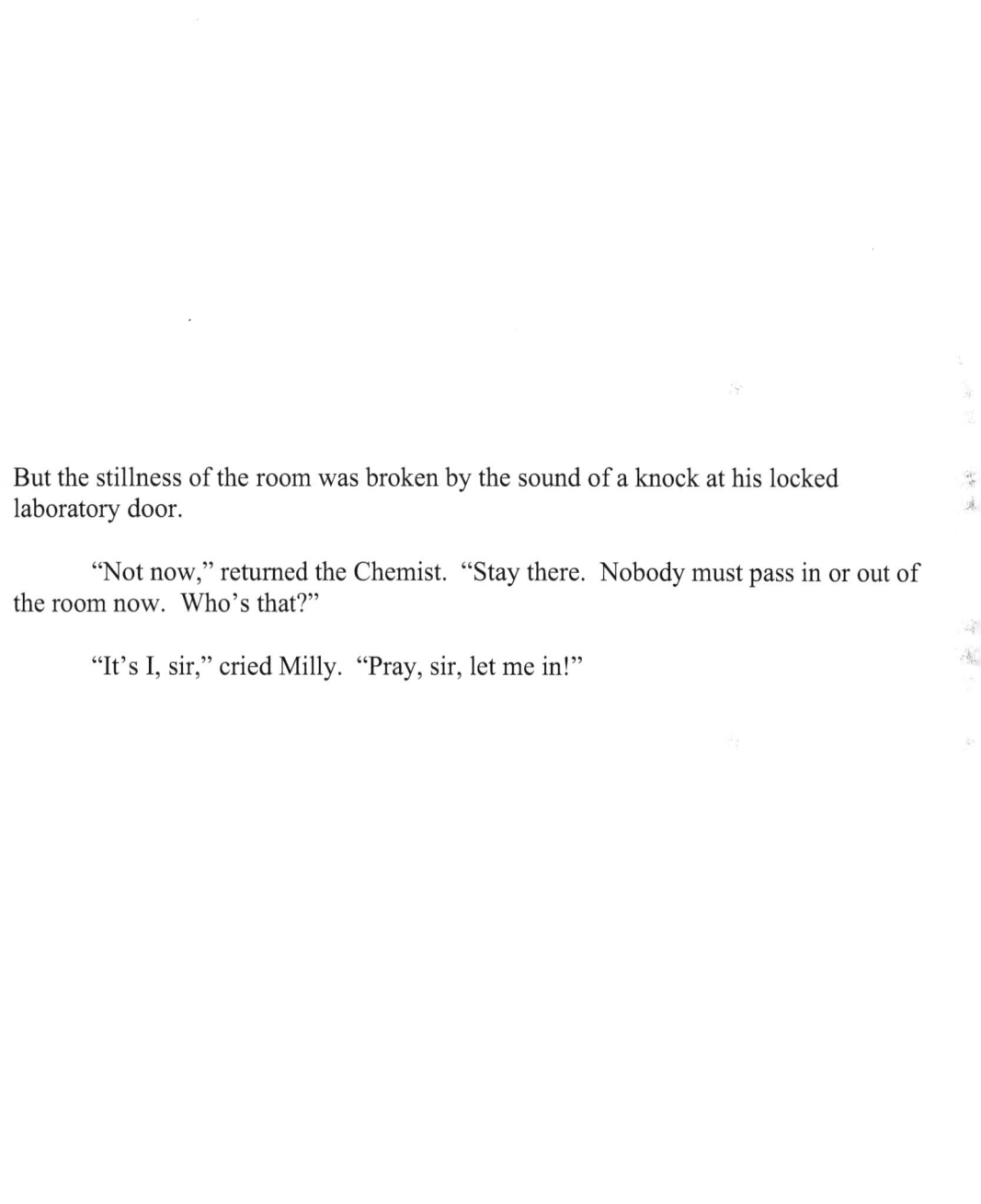

But the stillness of the room was broken by the sound of a knock at his locked laboratory door.

"Not now," returned the Chemist. "Stay there. Nobody must pass in or out of the room now. Who's that?"

"It's I, sir," cried Milly. "Pray, sir, let me in!"

III

"No! Not for the world!" he said.

"Mr Redlaw, Mr Redlaw, pray, sir, let me in."

"What is the matter?" he said, covering the student.

"I attended the sanatorium, sir, to visit poor George, but terrible news awaited me there! When I arrived, the police department were present. It seems George had suffered a delirium, no doubt caused by his declining sanity. He pushed his poor father and his dear brother from the window, after causing William great injury. It seems he could not wake himself from his terrible infatuation and, in a moment of madness, killed his father, brother and ultimately, himself. Oh, Mr Redlaw! They are all gone!"

"My dear, Milly," Redlaw shouted through the door, "Remain where you are. It is vitally important that you do not leave."

"But Mr Redlaw, yet further deeds were done this night, the most vile crimes I have ever heard tell. Oh, Mr Redlaw, pray advise me, help me!"

"No! Remain where you are!" he answered.

"Mr Redlaw! Dear sir! The student, Hobson had been muttering, in his doze, about you, who, he fears, would kill him. He said, in his wandering, that you came to him and bestowed a terrible plague upon him. Is this true? I spoke briefly to Mr Tetterby earlier tonight, but have heard nothing since. Is the poor boy well, sir? What is to be done? How is he to be saved? Mr Redlaw, pray, oh, pray, advise me! Help me!"

"Milly, you must trust in me. Remain by the door. Do not leave. You are in danger and I must help you!"

"As for the poor boy which I have fed these last few days, I returned home to find him slaughtered and a man examining his body."

Redlaw stopped. "A man?"

"He says he knows you, sir. Pray, let us in!"

All this time he struggled to find means to gag the restrained creature, and upon doing so covered him and opened the door a crack by which to see Milly.

Stood beside her was Herbert West.

"Phantoms! Punishers of impious thoughts!" cried Redlaw, gazing round in anguish, "look upon me! From the darkness of my mind, let the glimmering of contrition that I know is there, shine up and show my misery! In the material world as I have long taught, nothing can be spared; no step or atom in the wondrous structure could be lost, without a blank being made in the great universe. I know, now, that it is the same with good and evil, happiness and sorrow, in the memories of men. Pity me! Relieve me!"

Milly watched as Redlaw cried in horror, then responded with a cry, "Help! Let me in. He was your friend once, how shall he be followed, how shall he save us all? They are all changed, there is no one else to help me, pray, pray, let me in!"

West pushed his way through the gap in the door, pacing in to the room and quickly examining the specimen which lay restrained under the sheet.

Redlaw cried, "West, you must take this gift away! Or, if it must still rest with me, deprive me of the dreadful power of giving it to others. Undo what I have done. Leave me benighted, but restore the day to those whom I have cursed. As I have spared this woman from the first, and as I never will go forth again, but will die here, with no hand to tend me, save this creature who is proof against me, - hear me!"

Night was still heavy in the sky. On open plains, from hill-tops, and from the decks of solitary ships at sea, a distant low-lying line, that promised by-and-by to change to light, was visible in the dim horizon; but its promise was remote and doubtful, and the moon was striving with the night-clouds busily.

The shadows upon Redlaw's mind succeeded thick and fast to one another, and obscured its light as the night-clouds hovered between the moon and earth, and kept the latter veiled in darkness. Fitful and uncertain as the shadows which the night-clouds cast, were their concealments from him, and imperfect revelations to him; and, like the night-clouds still, if the clear light broke forth for a moment, it was only that they might sweep over it, and make the darkness deeper than before.

At such a time, Christmas music began to play outside. He listened to it at first, as he had listened in the church-yard; but presently - it playing still, and being borne towards him on the night air, in a low, sweet, melancholy strain - he rose, and stood stretching his hands about him, as if there were some friend approaching within his reach, on whom his desolate touch might rest, yet do no harm. As he did this, his face became less fixed and wondering; a gentle trembling came upon him; and at last his eyes filled with tears, and he put his hands before them, and bowed down his head.

His memory of sorrow, wrong, and trouble, had led him to this terrible bargain; he knew that West was incapable of reversing this bargain, nor ever would be. But some dumb stir within him made him capable, again, of being moved by what was hidden, afar off, in the music. If it were only that it told him sorrowfully the value of what he had lost, he thanked Heaven for it with a fervent gratitude.

As the last chord died upon his ear, he raised his head to listen to its lingering vibration. Beyond the student's corpse, Herbert West still stood, immovable and silent, with his eyes upon him.

Ghastly he seemed now, as he had ever been, but not so cruel and relentless in his aspect - or he thought or hoped so, as he looked upon him, trembling.

"Oh, tell me," exclaimed Redlaw, catching at the hope which he fancied might lie hidden in the words. "Can I undo what I have done?"

"No," returned West.

"I do not ask for restoration to myself," said Redlaw. "What I abandoned, I abandoned of my own free will, and have justly lost. But for those to whom I have transferred the fatal gift; who never sought it; who unknowingly received a curse of which they had no warning, and which they had no power to shun; can I do nothing?"

"Nothing," said West.

"If I cannot, can anyone?"

"You misunderstand me," West added, "There is nothing that can be done, for you have done nothing to them. Your gift bestowed, the bargain of life, was honestly given by me."

"You were wrong, West. Your research was flawed." Redlaw snapped at West, who shook his head.

West turned to Milly. "Show him," he told her.

Milly rolled up the sleeve of her blouse. Underneath, there was a large infection upon her arm that appeared to be shaped as a bite.

"I'm sorry, Mr Redlaw," Milly cried, "I didn't mean any harm. As William told you, my nature is kindly, and I only meant to help. William and Philip knew nothing. I kept her well hidden."

"Hidden?" Redlaw was confused, "Who?"

"Mrs Swidger has a guest whom she has hidden from her family for several months," West said. "Somebody who was very dear to you, Redlaw. I only wish that things has occurred differently."

Redlaw cried, "Surely, you can't mean…"

"It was William's sister, Mr Redlaw," Milly explained, "I found her, roaming the grounds the night following her burial. Fearing her to be a spectre, I kept my distance. But the following night, I encountered her again. She was ghastly, an unholy demon, but still she was William's sister. I couldn't bear for him to find her in such a condition and so I took her and hid her away. She was confused, aggressive. She attacked me, bit me on the arm. So I locked her away, malnourished and violent. I watched from a safe distance as she deteriorated over the weeks that followed, until she could not sustain herself any longer."

Milly wept and Redlaw sat stunned.

"The gift I bestowed upon you," West clarified, "was not responsible for the terrible plague. It manifested itself in Milly's bloodstream following her infected bite. The virus mutated over time. It was Milly who spread the infection."

Realisation dawned upon Milly, who became hysterical, "I killed them. They have all died and I am to blame. What now? What is to become of me?"

Redlaw and West were face to face again, and looking on each other, as intently and awfully as at the time of the bestowal of the gift, across Milly who lay weeping on the ground between them, at their feet.

"What is to be done?" asked Redlaw of West.

"This infection must be contained. I believe those who are most likely contaminated to be present in this room. It must not spread any further."

"And what of you?" Redlaw asked West.

West laughed, "I shall continue my research. Perhaps if I linger here long enough, I may see how effective your bestowed gift is, for it was the only measure of the solution I ever manufactured."

"Do you not seek to create more? To cure the human race of its suffering and pain, of loss and sorrow?" Redlaw recalled their conversation the previous night, of West's insistence of eradicating suffering through immortality.

"This experiment," said the West, pointing to Redlaw, "is the last, completest illustration of a human creature, utterly bereft of such cares as mortality. No softening memory of sorrow, wrong, or trouble enters here, because this wretched mortal from his birth has been abandoned to a worse condition than the beasts, and has, within his knowledge, no one contrast, no humanising touch, to make a grain of such a memory spring up in his hardened breast. All within this desolate creature is barren wilderness. All within the man bereft of what you have resigned, is the same barren wilderness. Woe to such a man! Woe, tenfold, to the nation that shall count its monsters such as this, lying here, by hundreds and by thousands!"

Redlaw listened, intently. West walked to the laboratory door and opened it, ready to depart.

"Behold, I say," pursued West, "the perfect type of what it was your choice to be. Your influence is powerless here, because from this you can banish nothing, nor could you ever have banished such a thing as beyond your design. Yet now, you must atone for the grief which led you to reanimate your unrequited love. Should there be aught for you to learn, it is not to be all consumed by such grief, but to channel it."

With that, West closed the door behind him and left Redlaw's lodgings, never to return.

Soon, now, the distant line on the horizon brightened, the darkness faded, the sun rose red and glorious, and the chimney stacks and gables of the ancient building gleamed in the clear air, which turned the smoke and vapour of the city into a cloud of gold. The very sun-dial in his shady corner, where the wind was used to spin with such unwindy constancy, shook off the finer particles of snow that had accumulated on his dull old face in the night, and looked out at the little white wreaths eddying round and round him. Doubtless some blind groping of the morning made its way down into the forgotten crypt so cold and earthy, where the stone arches were half buried in the ground, and stirred the dull sap in the lazy vegetation hanging to the walls, and quickened the slow principle of life within the little world of wonderful and delicate creation which existed there, with some faint knowledge that the sun was up.

The fire brigade attended to the building on Christmas morning. The blaze, it seemed, started from Redlaw's laboratory and consumed most of the crypt. The heat was so intense as to have turned much to ash. Investigators believed that Redlaw had been working with a student of his during the accident and a member of his staff, one Milly Swidger, was also present in the blaze. As to any connections with the horrific crimes that saw the death and subsequent consumption of both the remaining Swidger family members and the Tetterby family, none could be conclusively proven. Miskatonic University insisted, by means to prevent a spread of panic, that the deaths were unfortunate accidents, and as such were unrelated.

A grave was placed for Mr Redlaw in the grounds of the nearby cemetery, despite there being no discernible remains to bury, for the blaze made the establishing of such things a near impossibility. Yet stories remain to be told amongst the medical students of Miskatonic that Mr Redlaw did not die in the blaze that night.

In fact, it would be said for many years to come that a lone figure could be seen stalking the grounds of that particular building, every Christmas night, which bore an uncanny resemblance to the late Mr Redlaw.

Everybody said so.

Far be it from me to assert that what everybody says must be true. Yet, everybody said it looked like the haunted man

Glossary

Arkham - Arkham is a fictional city in Massachusetts, part of the Lovecraft Country setting created by H. P. Lovecraft and is featured in many of his stories. Arkham is the home of Miskatonic University, which figures prominently in many of Lovecraft's works

Azathoth - Azathoth is a deity in the Cthulhu Mythos and Dream Cycle stories of H. P. Lovecraft and other authors. The last major reference in Lovecraft's fiction to Azathoth was in 1935's "The Haunter of the Dark", which tells of "the ancient legends of Ultimate Chaos, at whose center sprawls the blind idiot god Azathoth, Lord of All Things, encircled by his flopping horde of mindless and amorphous dancers, and lulled by the thin monotonous piping of a demonic flute held in nameless paws."

Cthulhu - Lovecraft describes Cthulhu as "A monster of vaguely anthropoid outline, but with an octopus-like head whose face was a mass of feelers, a scaly, rubbery-looking body, prodigious claws on hind and fore feet, and long, narrow wings behind." Cthulhu has been described as a mix between a giant human, an octopus and a dragon, and is depicted as being hundreds of meters tall, with human-looking arms and legs and a pair of rudimentary wings on its back. "The Call of Cthulhu", was published in Weird Tales in 1928 and established the character as a malevolent entity hibernating within an underwater city in the South Pacific called R'lyeh. the imprisoned Cthulhu is apparently the source of constant anxiety for mankind at a subconscious level, and also the subject of worship by a number of religions.

Dagon - Father Dagon and his consort, Mother Hydra are both deep ones overgrown after millennia ruling over their lesser brethren. Together with Cthulhu, they form the triad of gods worshipped by the Deep Ones (their names are inspired by Dagon, the Semitic fertility deity, and the Hydra of Greek mythology). This group of gods is referenced in "At the Mountains of Madness," in which they waged a war against the Elder Things.

Deep Ones - The Deep Ones are a race of fish-frog-like, ocean-dwelling creatures with an affinity for mating with humans which occurs regularly along the coast. Numerous Mythos elements are associated with the Deep Ones, including the legendary town of Innsmouth, the undersea city of Y'ha-nthlei, the Esoteric Order of Dagon, and the beings known as Father Dagon and Mother Hydra.

Devil's Reef - In "The Shadow Over Innsmouth", Devil's Reef is located just off the coast of Massachusetts, near the town of Innsmouth. In Lovecraft's story, the U.S. government torpedoed Devil's Reef in 1928 as part of a raid on the town of Innsmouth. The undersea metropolis of Y'ha-nthlei is below the Reef.

Elder Things - The Elder Things were the first extraterrestrial species to come to the Earth, colonizing the planet about one billion years ago. They stood roughly eight feet tall and had the appearance of a huge, oval-shaped barrel with starfish-like appendages at both ends. On Earth, the Elder Things built huge cities, both underwater and on dry land.

Esoteric Order of Dagon - Esoteric Order of Dagon was the primary religion in Innsmouth after Captain Obed Marsh returned from the South Seas with the dark religion circa 1838. It quickly took root due to its promises of expensive gold artifacts and fish, which were desired by the primarily-fishing town. The central beings worshipped by the Order were the Deep Ones, Father Dagon, Mother Hydra, and, to a lesser extent, Cthulhu. The Deep Ones were seen largely as intermediaries between the various gods, rather than as gods themselves. Even so, the cultists sacrificed various locals to the Deep Ones at specific times in exchange for a limitless supply of gold and fish.

Innsmouth - Lovecraft writes that Innsmouth was "founded in 1643, noted for shipbuilding before the Revolution, a seat of great marine prosperity in the early nineteenth century, and later a minor factory centre." The loss of sailors due to shipwrecks and the War of 1812 caused the town's profitable trade with the South Seas to falter; by 1828, the only fleet still running that route was that of Captain Obed Marsh, the head of one of the town's leading families. In 1840, Marsh started a cult in Innsmouth known as the Esoteric Order of Dagon, basing it on a religion practiced by certain Polynesian islanders he had met during his travels. Shortly thereafter, the town's fishing industry experienced a great upsurge.

Miskatonic University - Miskatonic University is a university located in Arkham, a fictitious town in Essex County, Massachusetts. It is named after the Miskatonic River. After first appearing in the H. P. Lovecraft 1922 serial "Herbert West–Reanimator", the school appeared in numerous horror stories in the Cthulhu Mythos by Lovecraft and other writers. The story "The Dunwich Horror" implies that Miskatonic University is a highly prestigious university, on par with Harvard University, and that Harvard and Miskatonic are the two most popular schools for the children of the Massachusetts "Old Gentry".

Necronomicon – A grimoire. Among other things, the work contains an account of the Old Ones, their history, and the means for summoning them.

Old Ones - An ongoing theme in Lovecraft's work is the complete irrelevance of mankind in the face of the cosmic horrors that apparently exist in the universe, with Lovecraft constantly referring to the "Great Old Ones": a loose pantheon of ancient, powerful deities from space who once ruled the Earth and who have since fallen into a death-like sleep.

R'lyeh - According to Lovecraft's short story, R'lyeh is a sunken city in the South Pacific and the prison of the entity called Cthulhu.

Xoth - Xoth (or Zoth) is the green binary star where Cthulhu and his ilk once lived before coming to earth. According to the Xothic legend cycle, it is where Cthulhu mated with Idh-yaa to beget Ghatanothoa, Ythogtha, and Zoth-Ommog.

Y'ha-nthlei - In "The Shadow Over Innsmouth", it is described as a great undersea metropolis located below Devil's Reef just off the coast of Massachusetts, near the town of Innsmouth. Its exact age is not known, but one resident is said to have lived there for 80,000 years.

Printed in Great Britain
by Amazon